Have I Told You Lately?

MEN OF 3X CONSTRUCTION
BOOK ONE

By

Erosa Knowles

Have I Told You Lately?

Men of 3X Construction -Book one

The Men of 3X CONStruction have built a thriving business over the years and now someone is out to destroy not only their dream, but the men themselves. Our heroes won't stand for that any more than you or I would. They hook up with strong women, who help them stand stronger. In this series, we'll follow the unraveling thread to reveal the culprit and save the freedom of our heroes. Hopefully, the women will be able to calm the primitive natures within their men, lest they take the law into their own hands. Once in the cage, was enough.

Dedication

A special God Bless you to Linda and Jacqueline, excellent critique partners and esteemed writers themselves. The readers at The Valent Chamber, a rocking support group. My Editor: Elise Dee Beraru. As always my core group: Tristin, Christian, David and the home team, thanks for your strong-armed support.

Erosa Knowles- Men of 3X CONStruction
Book 1

Chapter 1

The loud crunching noise and subsequent spin happened so fast, Cherise's heart missed a couple of beats. Now that her car stopped, the organ banged double time against her ribcage. She placed her palm against her chest to keep it from breaking free.

The 2008 blue Accord spun in the middle of Fifteen Mile Road just past Big Rapids Senior High. Fortunately, it was the middle of the day and school hadn't let out yet. The weather was unseasonably warm, not bad for a Fall day in Michigan. Ferris State, her destination, was a few miles down the road. Close, but not close enough.

Cherise covered her face to keep from breathing the dust from the deployed side air bag and pushed open her car door. The highway shoulder lay a couple of footsteps away. She shivered in the breeze of a speeding car passing by. There was little shade; perspiration ran down her face and chest, irritating her eyes further. On wobbly legs, she moved to the side of her car and pitched forward. She flinched as a calloused hand took hold of her left arm.

"Don't touch me." The hoarseness of her vocal cords surprised her

A short, balding, older white male stood near her. Nausea and pain competed for her attention as she inhaled. Her heart dropped as she glanced at her mangled car while standing on the precipice of a major anxiety attack. After a year in therapy, she'd returned to college to finish her degree, confident in her ability to use the tools she'd learned in therapy to live as normal a life as possible.

Grappling her reserves, she pushed down the overwhelming fear threatening to choke her. There'd be no relapsing today or any day. Like a skilled surgeon, systematically she went through her cognitive restructuring drills. Her fingertips tapped the side of her car in concert with her pounding heart. Swallowing past the dust in her throat, she glanced up.

"Sorry, didn't mean to frighten you." He paused. "I'm Blake, by the way. Are you okay? Do I need to call an ambulance?" He squinted from the sun and waited.

Ignoring him and his question, she labored to breathe. If she didn't focus on her drills, she'd have a full-blown attack. And that wouldn't make anyone's day. She got busy with her exercise. "A car accident is a normal occurrence," she murmured. "People survive them every day, I will survive—"

A callused hand shook her shoulder. "Miss, I asked if you were okay."

"Do-not-touch-me." She spaced each word evenly as she bared her teeth and glared at the older man who entered her private space.

He dropped his hand as if she had two heads and was on fire. Both hands lifted, palms forward he backpedaled and then turned toward the F250 truck that had sideswiped her.

She'd apologize later and rubbed the spot he'd

touched. The buzz of a thousand bees drew her attention, a sure signal she'd lost ground. Her fist tightened as she forcibly slowed her breathing and the thundering of her heart.

"A simple accident," she muttered. "Everything's fine, it's okay." She took deep a few cleansing breaths and bent over, hands on thighs as she talked herself back from the brink of disaster.

"Miss, my name's Andre, I'm working here from out of town and I'm sorry for hitting your car. The light had turned green. I didn't see you coming through the red. The police are on their way. Is there anyone else we can call?" The smaller man walked from the passenger side of her car, it had curled like a soft pretzel from the impact of the heavier truck.

Thank goodness she'd had on her seatbelt. "I'm not sure exactly what happened." She peered up at him and then over to the light she'd drove through. "You're saying I ran the red light?" She'd been on her way to campus for an exam; it wasn't for a few hours. There hadn't been a need to rush.

"Yeah, I had the right of way on the green, and you drove through. Luckily you weren't driving too fast, the damage could've been worse." They glanced at her compact car. A few minutes ago, someone had pushed it to the side of the road. The passenger's seat lay tilted at an unnatural angle. That wasn't good.

Beneath lowered lids, she watched him. He stood near the hood of her car, hands pushed deep in his jeans. His furtive glances slid over her car and then the truck.

Erosa Knowles- Men of 3X CONStruction
Book 1

She tensed at his odd posturing.

Away from the dust, she breathed easier now. Wary, she glanced sideways and saw the older man, Blake, on the phone. Other cars had stopped; traffic slowed to a crawl, vaguely she remembered people talking to her through the windows earlier.

"Yeah, lucky me. I just paid the thing off and now it's probably totaled." She sucked her teeth and stretched. It was an effort, but she needed to get her car information for the police.

"Good, the bosses are here," Andre said, relief and something else threaded through his voice. He stiffened and moved slightly on the balls of his feet. "Don't worry Miss, Ross, Smoke or Red'll fix this right up, now that they're all here."

She couldn't be sure, but it sounded like he muttered "shit" under his breath as he walked off. The roar of engines and the accompanying dust caught her attention. The police had gotten there fast. She pushed away from her car, intent on getting her insurance and title information when her right leg buckled. She fell against the gravel. Tiny pebbles bruised her palm and knee.

"Ouch."

She struggled to stand. The need to be self-sufficient and handle this on her own without her parents' involvement remained front and center. Having your only child experience a debilitating disorder right after walking across the stage at graduation had marked her mom. After the year on the couch, she'd finally broken away, convinced of her cure. Her parents hadn't agreed, but she was twenty-five and in a position to make her own decisions.

"Don't move, I've got you." The deep voice left no room for argument.

In a smooth motion, her legs left the ground and she was placed on the supple leather of her front seat. A large hand gently touched her brow and heated face.

Instinctively, she moved back, the rough hand followed.

"She's warm, get the ambulance here now," he said. Feet scrambled outside the car. In the distance, she heard murmuring.

"I don't need a doctor. I'll be all right," she argued.

Dazed, the realization that he'd picked up her size sixteen body without hesitation penetrated. She pushed his hand away from her face with one hand, while pulling her sweatshirt down with the other. A quick brush against her hair assured her the shoulder-length ponytail kept hair from spiraling all over her head. Satisfied she didn't look like an asylum escapee, she closed her eyes allowing her thoughts to turn to this new dilemma.

"Sure thing. Look at me."

She opened her eyes. Large hazel ones probed. He nodded.

"Maybe not a fever, but you're running warm. Maybe you should let a doctor check you out to be sure." He paused giving her a quick look over. "What happened just now? Did you hurt your leg in the accident?"

"I'm not sure." She licked dry lips, checking out his jeans, tee and flannel over-shirt. "You aren't the police. Who are you?

Erosa Knowles- Men of 3X CONStruction
Book 1

"Ross Stemple. I work for the company whose truck hit yours. Red, bring me a bottle of water from the ice chest on the back of my truck," he called, without turning. His hands encompassed hers.

The mention of water reminded her of the dust from the airbag. Dizziness assailed her as the smell of the dust penetrated. She leaned back into the seat. Even the persistent buzzing noise seemed far away. The sun must've ducked behind a cloud, since the day seemed darker. Her head felt heavy and light. A strange feeling enveloped her.

He squeezed her hand.

"Stay with me. Here, drink this. Let's get you hydrated."

His voice held an odd mixture of compassion and authority penetrating the fog in her head. Her tongue searched for moisture. Ross placed a cold bottle into her warm palms and wrapped her hands around it. A tingling sensation radiated up her arms. He twisted off the cap and held her hands, with the bottle, and placed it near her mouth.

She gasped the moment the cold liquid touch her lips. Her mouth opened wider and she drank greedily, clearing her mind somewhat. After draining the bottle, she opened her eyes and leaned further back.

"Thank you," she stammered.

Uncertainty rifled through her. A large white man crouched in front of her on the side of the road. Covertly she watched him, appreciating his unhurried movements as he stood and disposed of the bottle. She liked his aura of command. He wore a baseball cap backward over shoulder length dark brown hair. A cropped close beard hugged his angular face. She pegged him for late twenties, early thirties. His wide chest and muscular arms created an interesting package. She couldn't make out the pattern of the tattoo on his shoulder, but the dark swirling colors caught her eye.

He glanced at the passenger side of her car. "Do you remember what happened?"

"Very little. I'd just received a text and picked up my cell when the truck hit me. At least I think that's what happened. The small man, Andre I think he introduced himself." She pointed in the direction of the truck where the man leaned indolently, "said I ran the red light."

His head followed her hand, nodded and returned. "Are you sure you're okay?"

"Just a little dizzy. But I think I will see a doctor. My leg gave out and that's never happened before." She rubbed the offending limb.

"Miss?" His brow rose.

She eyed him before answering. "Cherise Walters."

"Cherise, can you see under the passenger's seat?" His voice sounded stilted as he nodded in the direction of the upturned chair.

She turned to look. "Yeah, pretty much." It looked like it had rained dusty pencils. The front floorboard was covered with her large stash of sharpened pencils and airbag dust. Warmth crept up her cheek. How would she explain that many pencils? Two, five or maybe even ten for an exam, but a bag of fifty wasn't normal. She bit her lip and tried to think of a plausible explanation.

Erosa Knowles- Men of 3X CONStruction
Book 1

"Do you see that small manila envelope on the floor?"

"What? An envelope?" Surprise over his question erased her embarrassment. She twisted further. "Oh yeah, I see it now. What is it?"

"It's yours, isn't it?" His voice sounded skeptical.

"No, I've never seen it before. What is it?" She reached over to pick it up. He caught her arm. She looked at him. "Why'd you do that?" She asked, wondering what was going on. He'd just drove up, so why was he so interested in a small envelope?

"You don't know what it is, it could be something harmful."

"Okay, but it's in my car." She drew out the words, as she watched him carefully. "How'd it get there?" She hated the confusion lacing her tone. Now that he'd brought it up, she needed answers and didn't understand where he was going with all this.

He rose. "Excuse me." He reached past her and picked it up. After a second of squeezing and running his finger over the closed envelope, he sighed.

"What? What is it?" Her mind started whirling, filling in blanks of what could be in the small packet. None of it made sense.

"Who came to that side of your car?"

"Who?" Her voice rose. "I don't know, people stopped and asked questions. I couldn't tell you who came to the car." She reached for the envelope; he pulled it out of reach.

"Look you'd better tell me what's in that envelope or I'll be calling the police." This was not the time or the day to play guessing games. Her nerves huddled loosely together but could break wide open any minute.

He gazed at her for a moment and then nodded. "You should do that, call the police. I'm not sure what's inside since I haven't opened it, but it feels like some type of powder, possibly cocaine. From the thickness of it, there's quite a bit. Street value would probably be pretty high." He opened his palm handing her the envelope.

Cherise's mouth gaped in surprise. What had she expected him to say? She had no idea but certainly not that. "Cocaine? As in drugs? Did you say drugs?" She whispered as shock reverberated through her frame. The calm from the accident shattered. Her legs trembled as fine tremors shook her core. The buzzing in hr head returned thunderously. She leaned forward, lightheaded, dizzy. Her throat closed tight, she couldn't breathe.

Jail, she was going to jail.

"Inhale, take your time, pull in small sips of air."

He pushed her head down toward her thighs. After a few breaths the nausea slowed, air returned gradually, the gray borders thinned and the fluttering sounds receded. Strong hands stroked her back in a circular pattern, lending warmth and a sense of security during what had been a frightful moment.

"I don't do drugs. I've never even seen cocaine." She shivered beneath his palm. "That's not my envelope." She prayed he believed her, since the police were on their way. They wouldn't ask questions first, they'd take her to jail. *Ohmigod, jail.* Her breath hitched.

"I know. Look," he said, shaking the envelope in

Erosa Knowles- Men of 3X CONStruction
Book 1

front of her. "It's not buried in the dust from the airbag. That's why I asked who came to the passenger side of your car." His finger lifted her chin. She stared into a pool of hazel brown certainty. "I'm not sure what's going on here or why. Did anyone from the truck lean or reach into the passenger side of your car?"

The question rattled her mind. Several people came and looked around the car. The hit happened on the passenger side. But did anybody reach in? She couldn't recall. "I'm sorry. I don't remember if they leaned in or not."

He nodded and handed her the envelope.

She stared at the viperous package and shook her head. "I don't want that." She pushed his hand away.

He took her hand in his. "What if I'm wrong and it's a gift for you. Money or something your boyfriend left in your car."

She snorted derisively, and pulled away, brushing her hands. "Not possible. No boyfriend and no one I know would use an envelope like that for a card or gift. No, I don't want whatever's in that package. Get rid of it."

He glanced at her.

"Please."

He nodded, stood and yelled, "Smoke."

For the first time she realized just how tall and muscular her rescuer was. He moved the cap from his head and ran his hand through his hair. He replaced the cap as a dark brother sauntered over to her car. She stared at the newcomer's low cut hair and gold hoop earring. He reminded her of a beefed up Miami Heat basketball player, Dwayne Wade, except he was only a little over six feet by her estimation. What did these men do to have bodies like these?

"Cherise, this is my partner Smoke. Smoke—Cherise." He nodded to each during the introductions. "I found this in her car on top of everything, by the passenger seat." He held the envelope so his partner would be the only one viewing it.

"Hmmm," Smoke said before looking at her again. "Are you okay, Cherise? The truck did some serious damage to your car."

She blinked. Did he ask about her injury instead of dealing with the envelope? "Yes, although I plan to get checked out after the police get here." She stressed police, hoping he'd understand the seriousness of the matter. If she hadn't seen them pull up, she might suspect a sinister plot of some sort. Even now, her obsessive mind calculated the odds of their involvement.

"Good, they should be here any minute." Smoke nodded. "What do you plan to do about the envelope? Why haven't you opened it? Do you know what's inside?" His calm, matter of fact questioning eased her rising tension.

"No." She pointed to his partner. "Ross, I believe you said your name was."

He nodded.

"Ross saw it under the seat and has some suspicions." She looked around before whispering. "He thinks it may be drugs and I don't do drugs. I told—," She inhaled to fight her rising panic. "I asked him to get rid of it for me before the police came."

Erosa Knowles- Men of 3X CONStruction
Book 1

"Why would he do that? Don't you think the cops would want to check the it out?" He shrugged, looked at the envelope and then back at her. "It may not be what you think."

"Yeah, right. Since when did they start giving us a fair shot? Blacks always get taken to jail first and questioned later," she snapped losing patience with his calm attitude. Her world was collapsing and he asked silly questions.

The men looked at each other.

Smoke crouched in front of her. She hadn't seen when he'd taken the envelope, but it lay on his palm. "Cherise, I hope for your sake you're not playing my friend or me." He opened the envelope and shook it gently. White powder spilled to the lip of the packet.

She shrank back. "What is it?"

Smoke dipped his pinky into the powder and tasted it. "Salt."

"Salt?" Her voice shook. "Thank goodness." She breathed noisily as moisture filled her eyes. "I've never been so scared in my life." The sounds of a siren blared in the background. She relaxed and lay backward. An engine roar caught her attention. She peered around Ross, as a truck took off down the road.

"Where's Smoke going?"

The police pulled in behind her damaged car.

Ross turned and stared. "It wasn't salt."

Chapter 2

Ross was far from home. This job in Big Lakes, and many like them, took him to various parts of the Midwest. Living at extended stay hotels was a way of life, and a price he willingly paid in pursuit of his dream.

He took in the sights and smells of the jobsite. The tall stacks of wood, various sizes of pipes, stone and mortar, a few basic ingredients for an eventual masterpiece. Normally, construction sites filled him with peace and satisfaction. Today had been a narrow escape. As part-owner of a thriving construction company that hired ex-convicts, he was vigilant to keep even the illusion of criminal activity far from their workplace. He'd noticed the dust-free envelope immediately after placing Cherise on the seat of her car. The fact she hadn't noticed it or seen anything wrong eased his mind. Dealing with druggies complicated matters.

Andre walked toward him. The man had been working for them a month, fresh from Michigan's Prison Building Program. Rubie, his mentor, had praised Andre's carpentry skills. So far, they hadn't had any problems with his work, but someone *had* stashed drugs in that car. There had been more than enough for resale. Worse, his men, both ex-cons, were on the scene. With all their recent problems with suppliers, and miscalculations on jobsites, having the police bust one of his men for drugs was a PR nightmare they didn't need. Removing the packet from the scene of the accident benefited everyone, although he didn't tell Cherise. He smiled thinking of her probable reaction. She was a spitfire. Despite her fear, she tossed out demands and held her ground. The cops would've had a fight on their hands for real if Smoke hadn't taken away the packet.

"Sorry about the accident, Boss. I swear her car came out of nowhere, I swerved to miss hitting her head on, and caught the side." Andre talked around a toothpick in his mouth.

"It's okay. The police gave her the ticket based on the tire marks and the swipe on her car. The truck had little damage. Make sure you clean up your area before we stop for the day. Tomorrow we need to make up for the time lost earlier." He slapped the smaller man on the shoulder before walking away.

Jake Smalley, one of the security officers watching their site, waved Ross over. "Hey, Ross."

"What's up?" The two men shook hands.

"Nothing much, I just wanted to check in with you make sure everything's good before you lock down for the night."

"Everything's good. Just make sure it stays that way. We have serious inventory locked up here. Mrs. Frenche will hurt you if anything happens to her custom lights or stair railing." He smiled at the older man's look of horror at the mention of the owner's wife.

"Sure thing," he stuttered before running to the car and jumping in.

Ross laughed as the man gunned the engine and drove to the rear of the lot where the containers were located.

Red and Smoke, his partners owning an equal share of the company, met him in the middle of the lot. "You need to stop teasing him about Mrs. Frenche. She scares the piss out of him." Smoke nodded at the dust from the car as Ross's laughter died off.

"What do you think?" Red asked looking around the site.

"About?" Ross glanced at Smoke, who nodded. Damn, that meant he'd clued Red in on the drugs in the woman's car.

"The sun in the fucking sky," Red snapped, glaring at him. "Did Andre or Ollie put the drugs in the car? 'Cuz I got a good look at that l'il Black Beauty and she's not a user."

"Naw, she's not a user." Smoke spit on the ground.

Ross hated when he did that, and his partner knew it.

"I saw the relief in her eyes when I told her it was salt." Smoke chuckled.

"You shitting me? Salt?' Red laughed and pushed Smoke's shoulder. "She couldn't tell the difference between powder and granules?"

"Needed to see her reaction, it worked." Smoke cupped his hand and lit a cigarette. The three of them watched the activity around the site.

"Andre," Red said decisively. "If one of our men planted the coke, it'd be him. He's still nervous as a bee around honey; he knows we'd never release him for an accident like that. Besides, she was at fault. What's he got to be nervous about now?"

"Why not Ollie?" Smoke countered. "He abused back

in the day."

"Not since he married his old lady," Red said. "Heard she put her foot down and he's been clean for years."

"What if someone put it there before the accident and neither of our men is guilty?" Ross asked, as they walked toward their trucks for privacy. The wheels of speculation turned.

"There are too many variables and not enough information," Ross continued. "I agree she's not a user, but somebody she knows may be. What if she gave a friend a ride and they stashed the powder until they could pick it up later?"

Ross took off his cap, allowing the light breeze to cool him. "But, that doesn't explain why the envelope was dust free."

"Maybe it slid from under the seat after the dust settled. Only a fool would leave that much powder under a seat without making sure it stayed put." Red scoffed. "But then again, some people don't think that far ahead."

Smoke agreed. "That's a definite possibility, but it doesn't feel right. No matter. If it was a friend or someone from the accident, the powder's gone. Let's hope no one comes looking for it."

Red whistled. "Black Beauty could be in a lot of trouble, coke ain't cheap and someone might try and mess her up."

"Or," Smoke said. "They'd come looking for the person she last saw with the envelope. I think it's safe to assume that if one of our men stashed the drugs, it was temporary until after the police left the scene. They can't afford to be caught dirty."

"Right," Ross said, watching the hustle around them. "Nor could they afford for us to track the drugs back to them. Automatic dismissal."

"What you're saying is, if one of our men stashed the drugs in the car, then this incident's over." Red looked at them as he spoke. "He won't retaliate. But if not, there could be some blow back on Black Beauty and possibly Smoke." He nodded in the man's direction.

Smoke pulled on his cigarette and blew the smoke out the side of his mouth. "No question, there was enough powder for serious financial gain. Unfortunately, it's in the lake now, courtesy of the sewer."

"You flushed it?" Red asked, incredulously.

Smoke nodded. "Sheeit, I couldn't afford to have it on me either or anywhere around here. I went to McDonalds, flushed the powder, washed the envelope and threw it away."

Ross nodded. "Even though it's a long shot that one of our men had drugs on them, let's keep an eye on them anyway. I'm not happy over some invoices we've received lately. Some bids have gone down wrong and weird stuff's been happening." He deliberately kept his tone neutral; they'd have to meet soon over some troubling paperwork.

Smoke sent him a searching look.

He ignored it.

"For real," Red said. 'We've worked too long and hard to let some punks mess over us now. I've been tightening up on my crew and their waste. I got on them twice this week about throwing out things before they're used up." He nodded toward his team of plumbers and drywallers.

"The real drag is we're not getting the same quality of workers from the building program like we did at first," Smoke said. "I talked to Rubie about it and he said all these assholes received the same training and we should be patient. I swear, if I have to explain what *on center* means to somebody else, I'm firing his ass. And Rubie can kiss mine."

Ross nodded. "When we have dinner with him tomorrow, make sure you let him know what problems we're having with these men he sent. As much as we owe Rubie, we won't take sorry workers. He's helped a lot of people through the program. But somebody's off their game."

Red snorted. "The last few men he sent would rather drink and lay around all day. They don't want to work. I don't understand it."

"Didn't Andre come within the past two months?" Smoke asked.

They turned and watched the smaller man as he loaded Red's truck. "Yep," Red said. "I have to stay on him. He takes too many cigarette breaks. The other men haven't taken to him yet. He eats alone and stays to himself."

Ross glanced at his cell, turned and walked toward his truck.

"Yo boss, where you headed?" Red called out.

"I've got a date."

"A date? Now?" Red asked, his face scrunched in confusion.

Smoke smiled, waved and walked off.

"Yeah, talk to you later." Ross waved, jumped in his truck and headed for the emergency clinic in town. Cherise was ready to leave.

She'd shrieked after his salt announcement. When the police asked what was wrong, she'd told them her leg hurt. She'd agreed to a trip to the clinic with the condition he'd pick her up after the examination and explain what was going on. It'd been an easy compromise since he knew little more than she did.

When he pulled into the circular driveway of the facility, he saw her pecan brown face peering through the double glass doors. He smiled as he walked in. She leaned against the counter talking to an older woman. Slanted, dark chocolate eyes, set in a heart-shaped face, watched his progress. The minx lowered long lashes in a coy move and blinked.

He chuckled at the unspoken challenge. He'd been attracted to her from the first. Earlier when he'd picked her up by her car, the fragrance of peaches mixed with the talcum from the airbag tugged at his base nature. His response to her surprised him, and that didn't happen often. This challenge he planned to win.

She turned from the counter and smiled at him. A surge of warmth filled him. Her dusty ponytail drooped around her long neck as she hobbled forward.

"Thanks for picking me up. I talked to my agent and someone will deliver a rental car later today. So I'm all set." She waved to the attendant as she walked out the door.

Erosa Knowles- Men of 3X CONStruction
Book 1

Remembering her reaction from before, he allowed her space to move. Her head barely reached his chest, and at six three, that placed her somewhere around five seven or eight. His eyes traveled down her back, lingering over her high round ass and long shapely legs, which snagged his attention earlier. Even with the streaks of dust, he'd thought her pretty. Cleaned up, he revised his opinion. She was beautiful.

"It's no problem; we're finished for the day. Too much excitement." He laughed at her arched brow and opened the truck. After a minute of watching her try to avoid hitting her sore leg, he lifted her and sat her in the passenger side, ignoring her yelp.

"You should've asked," she sassed, while cutting her eyes at him.

He grinned and walked to his side of the truck. *Oh yeah, she's interested.*

Chapter 3

After leaving the clinic, Cherise needed to reschedule the exam she'd missed earlier that day. Ross drove her across campus to her professor's office. After she tracked down the graduate assistant and secured an actual date for the test, she was in a much better frame of mind.

"My insurance agent didn't sound too promising when I called about the accident. They'll probably total it. My rental will be ready later today and they'll deliver it to the apartment."

Now that her "must do's" were taken care of, she was nervous. He'd been nice so far, but he was a stranger and she didn't know how to act. For starters, he was white. Nice tan, nice body, and nice smile, but still white. Old insecurities resurfaced. What did he think about the pencils in the car? She'd never been alone, well in a car, with any man outside her race.

Her face heated at her mind's direction. It's not as if he'd shown interest in her as a woman. Except when he stared at her a little too long at the clinic, or when he touched her face a little longer than necessary at the accident. And why did he insist he'd pick her up from Urgent Care? Her analytical mind argued forgetting their compromise. After all, she'd been at fault in the accident; his company didn't owe her anything.

"You mentioned that earlier."

"Oh, right, sorry." She hunched her shoulders and looked out the windows as more warmth suffused her face.

"Are you hungry?"

Starved, more like it. "No, I'm good. I have something at the apartment I'm going to warm up so I can take the pain pills. I swear I hurt more now that they've pushed and pulled than at the accident."

He nodded and smiled.

Her obsessive mind created, scrapped and recreated a dozen scenarios of a woman alone in a car with a stranger. Squeezing her palms together in her lap, she cursed her overactive brain when ten minutes later; they pulled into her parking lot. He hopped from the truck and opened her door. Despite her injury, she refused to let him carry her. He assisted her up the steps to her one bedroom apartment.

"Thanks again, Ross. You've been very nice considering I damaged your company's truck." She remembered her shock when Ross informed the police he was co-owner of the construction company. He'd said the black guy, Smoke, was his partner. The other partner, Red reminded her of the incredible hulk as he stood to the side talking to some men. He was taller than Ross and wider. All three men could be poster boys for "Men your mama yelled, "Run" on sight." She felt duly notified; they were what her mama'd call 'big leaguers'. Never in a million years would she have put the three of them together. And definitely not with a company that had at least four top of the line huge trucks.

"That's what insurance is for; it'll be taken care of." He opened her door. "I'd like to take you to dinner one night."

She frowned at his out of the blue invitation. "Why? I hit your truck. You don't owe me anything." She stopped inside her door and looked at him, gauging his seriousness.

"Why?" He stared at her. "To eat, talk; get to know each other better. Normally, that's what people do at dinner."

They stared at each other for a moment.

Normal, her main goal in life. A restful and quiet mind, instead of peaks of irrational fear. No more sleepless nights, sharp chest pains, or shortness of breath at the weirdest moments. Simple things so many people took for granted.

In contrast, a quiet dinner in a nice restaurant with a nice person sounded good. It couldn't hurt, and might be an opportunity for her to strengthen her social skills.

"Can I call you?" she said instead. Today had been full of surprises and she needed to settle down before she made any commitments.

"Sure." He handed her his business card. "Call me soon, Cherise." He tapped the tip of her nose and walked away.

###

A pounding head and scratchy eyes greeted Ross Monday morning. With measured steps, he moved in a deliberate direction to the shower. First, a cold water to snap him awake. Next, he cranked the dial in the opposite direction. Hot water to bathe. He took a trick from Scooby-do and shook off the water before taking a towel.

Now that he was awake—and alert—a thought

cleared the sticky webs left over from sleep. Cherise hadn't called. She'd surprised him. His control over factors in his life was such that surprises were rare and unwelcome. His mind whirred as he mulled over his conversation with her. In a bizarre twist, her not following his script made her more interesting. He wondered why she'd blown him off and how she'd take him showing up at her apartment. She'd be pissed. That thought made him smile. Idly he pulled out the plans and started coffee.

A few moments later, Red and Smoke knocked. Their suites were down the hall.

"Mornin," he said opening the door.

"Mornin." Each mumbled as they walked inside.

"Coffee's ready, plans on the table, go ahead and get started."

Both men grabbed a cup of coffee and sat at the table as he walked in the bedroom. Ross returned dressed in his trademark jeans, flannel shirt and tee, carrying a notepad. After grabbing a cup and resetting the coffee maker, he joined them for their morning meeting.

"We made real progress on the exterior walls for the first floor yesterday. We need to finish the interior wall studs and start on the second floor before lunch. Smoke, your team starts here. Red, you guys here and I'll take this area," he said pointing at the specs. "I figure we should have the first floor finished within an hour. Then we'll start with the joists for the second floor. Red, you start with the walls for the second floor while Smoke and I get the joists done. That way we'll save time." He pointed to the various sections as he talked.

"What time will the crane come to set the trusses?"

Smoke asked, while looking over the framing plans.

"Connie confirmed — "Ross stopped at the sound of his phone. Glimpsing the caller ID, he smiled and held up a finger as he walked away from the table.

"I know we agreed you'd call me soon, that was Friday," he said in a low voice cradling the phone.

"You *told* me to call you soon. I acknowledged your request. At any rate, I'm calling now." She paused." I can go to dinner Wednesday. Will that work for you?"

He smiled at her nervousness. A part of him reveled in her shyness. His protective nature rose to the forefront winning the battle against his inner dog. With his back to his partners, he answered. "Wednesday will be good." His voice lowered, "tonight would be better."

"Un-huh. Maybe for you, but I'm trying to graduate in a few months and have to stay on my game. Look at how early I'm calling. No one in their right mind is up before seven AM." She paused. "Oh Lord, I did it again. I'm being rude. You're up and I do believe you're in your right mind. I'm just…forget I said that."

He laughed. Their upbeat conversation presented a godsend. Her laughter chased the doldrums from last evening into the morning sun. Last night, he'd been tense over material losses, some other turnovers, the numbers weren't adding up and yes, he'd expected her call.

"Riiight, laughing at me, not very polite. You're supposed to ignore my outbursts like a gentleman."

"Hey, I never claimed to be a gentleman, and I'm getting ready to walk out the door for work. In my right mind, for sure."

Erosa Knowles- Men of 3X CONStruction
Book 1

She groaned.

"Hey, it's all good. I'll call you later today."
Checking behind him, Smoke and Red refilled their cups with grins on their faces.

"All right, hold on I'll give you my phone number. I never dial it, so I have it written down somewhere. Give me a second."

"Cherise," he called. "Cherise."

"Huh?"

"Your number showed up on my caller ID. I have it."

"Oh… yeah that's right. You see it *is* too early. I'm hanging up now. Have a good day."

"You, too." He chuckled when he realized he spoke to air.

"Hmmm, Cherise. What's up?" Smoke asked.

Ross glanced at his watch. Although the call had been important for his frame of mind, the team was running behind schedule. Smoke and Red waited for the morning briefing *and* new tidbits. He needed to complete both in ten minutes.

"That was Cherise."

"Black Beauty from the accident last week?" Red asked.

He nodded. "Her name's Cherise, use it."

Chapter 4

Cherise met Ross at the local seafood restaurant. Shrimp and salmon had been weaknesses of hers since childhood. She requested a seat in the heated glass arbor in the rear of the sea creature themed eatery.

Twilight was her favorite time of day. The sun said good-bye and the moon kissed you hello. She never tired of gazing at the sky. It settled something within her. Her mind quieted in tribute, offering a respite from the tension of her day.

A natural park faced the rear of the building. Trees of all shapes and sizes stood as sentinels, feeding, protecting plant and animal life nearby. As she looked out the large bay windows of the restaurant into the dark evening, a sense of serenity blanketed her. If only she could capture and bottle this moment, peace on demand she'd call it.

Turning in her chair; her eyes collided with Ross's. After a momentary stare down, her eyes slid to another table where a couple shared a glass of wine and talked quietly.

"Okay, why are you staring at me? It's not like this is a blind date. What's up with that?" She groaned. People staring made her nervous. When she got nervous, her mouth and mind disconnected. Hence, the blurting of private thoughts.

She covered her face with one hand while he chuckled. "Great, I'm just a big source of amusement. I'm gone." Placing one hand on the table, she started to rise.

Erosa Knowles- Men of 3X CONStruction
Book 1

His hand clamped over hers, holding her in place.

"First off, you're sexy, pretty, and woman you're *wearing* that dress." His eyes roved over the rust-colored sleeveless outfit.

Warmth and pride suffused her at his words. For the past year and a half, she'd exercised constantly while practicing her cognitive drills. She would never be a size five, never had for that matter. But a shapely size sixteen worked with her five feet seven frame. Her friends called her statuesque.

"Your hair, smile, quite a package," he continued. "I can't help but stare." He licked his lips slowly as his eyes dropped to her considerable breasts.

She smiled graciously. No need for him to know she'd changed her mind on her dress a dozen times, or how she'd grappled with how to wear her thick mane all day. She'd finally chosen the slinky low-cut dress to highlight her dark complexion and curves. Her hair she wore down so that it brushed her face and hit her back in a soft curl. Everything had to be perfect. Glancing at the appreciation in his eyes, she was glad her peculiarities paid off for once. The gleam of approval from him signaled mission accomplished.

"You *are* beautiful. Second, I'm not laughing at you. I like it when you say what you feel, less bullshit to wade through. Third, please don't leave. I promise to try and not stare, but damn, I'm just a man." He made a woeful expression while his hand grabbed his chest.

She laughed. Her heart soared. Everything would be fine.

###

"The lovely Ms. Cherise looked good, man. Where's she from?" Red asked as they walked into Ross's suite later that evening.

"I'm not sure. We haven't gotten to family stuff yet. You're right, though. She looked hot tonight. When she walked into the restaurant, I didn't recognize her at first," Ross said over his shoulder while picking up his dirty tee-shirt from the sofa.

"I hope you didn't say that to her."

"Nah, man, I'm not crazy. It was her sexy butt. I remembered that and walked over."

"How come you didn't remember her? The accident was only a few days ago." Red walked to the refrigerator and pulled out a beer. He offered it to Ross, who declined. They both slumped on the sofa.

"When I met her, she had airbag dust on her face, in her hair, some shirt, and jeans. Nothing like that sweet clingy dress tonight." He shook his head in awe over the luscious Cherise. He wanted her more now than before. She was the perfect size for him with the right amount of meat on her bones. As a big man, he required a woman with some cushion, and she fit perfectly under his arm.

"Was she surprised when you brought her to the pool hall after dinner?" Red asked breaking the silence.

Ross stroked his bearded face. "No, at least not that I could tell. I wasn't sure I would bring her at first. But we got to talking and I wanted the evening to go a l'il longer, spend more time with her. You feel me?"

"She looked classy, man." Red tipped his beer can and stared at him.

Erosa Knowles- Men of 3X CONStruction
Book 1

"Yeah, that's what I was thinking."

"You're not going to be able to tap that and run. You know that, right?"

"Yeah, kind of came to me tonight when she and Smoke talked about education and college. She's smart and all about her life's plans and goals. I realize that." Ross wiped his face with the palm of his hand.

"Question—you ready for that? You ready for a one on one? Because I think that's the price of admission for that lady."

"No... maybe. I don't know. I mean hell, we're here for what? Two, three months. I wasn't looking for anything serious. But damn, she's fine, smart and nice. I like that. You ever mess with a nice girl? A good girl?"

Red looked up at the ceiling. "Yeah, didn't work out. I still think about her though."

Ross knew he talked about the mother of his twins, Denise. He'd forgotten about her since she never came around anymore.

"I'm not sure what I'mma do." Ross said, changing the subject back to Cherise. "I'm supposed to call her tomorrow. On the real side, we keep talking and hanging out, I'm gonna tap it, and maybe brand it." He frowned in concentration, uncertain of his actions. She was different. There were elements of strength and fragility about her that pulled at him viscerally.

"You brand it, you own it. Be careful." Red warned him. "Shit, you might be the one who gets caught up. You ever think of that. She might turn you out."

"Could be man, I doubt it, but you could be right." He waited for the cold sweat to hit, or hives from that announcement. Nada. None of the normal mockery or flashes of fear. He was in stasis, a wait-see kind of thing. As a make-things-happen guy, his present state sucked.

He stretched out on the sofa and turned on the TV to give his mind a rest. The business took its toll; so many things had been going wrong lately. Maybe Cherise was just the distraction he needed.

Red's cell went off. He whooped and hollered before he answered it. "What's up, Felicia?" His slow, even voice at odds with his earlier action.

Ross's brow rose in surprise, "Felicia?" He mouthed, thinking of the woman from the Subway sandwich joint. Red had been after her for weeks.

His partner nodded and checked his pocket for keys and signaled later.

Ross nodded and continued flipping channels. The night had started with promise, but right now alone on in his place it seemed pathetic. Pathetic and lonely, two words he didn't ever associated with his. Determined not to be alone, he left and went to the corner bar where he could pretend at least he wasn't lonesome.

Chapter 5

Cherise's favorite movie watched her as she sat in her small living room chronicling her journal about her date. She'd stared at his casual dress as he took her hand and led her to their table.

Ross's nice round ass filled his jeans; he wore a funky urban shirt and large decorated jeans.

She sighed as risqué thoughts flashed through her mind. The man was hot.

It took him a few minutes, but he'd been able to draw her into an entertaining conversation. They shared a love for many of the same R&B singers and he knew more about a few of them. His vocabulary was an interesting mix of perfect grammar and slang. He'd flip from one to the other with an ease she appreciated. The man cussed too much, and she'd mentioned it. She doubted he'd change.

No question, tonight, her perceptions of white men took a beating. Granted, her list had been short, her experience nil. But she'd heard her friends talk back in college. College, she flinched. Receiving her BA seemed like decades ago instead of the two years it'd been. The shrill ring of her cell reminded her she needed to get some new ring tones, maybe something with a jazzy beat. Anything would be better than what she had. With an air of expectation, she picked up the device and looked at the caller ID. Her shoulders slumped.

Mama.

Not that she expected a call from Ross, that was a lie.

She'd have enjoyed talking to him a little more. He had a quirky sense of humor and she found his keen intelligence sexy. More than once tonight she'd been amazed by his insight, his ability to cut through the fat to get to the important meat of a situation.

"Hi, mama."

"Whew, a little more enthusiasm and you'll bowl me over, baby girl."

She laughed. "Sorry, just sitting here reflecting on a few things."

"On a Wednesday night? I thought school was on track. Everything okay?"

The worry in her mother's voice stiffened her spine. The last thing she wanted was her mama traveling to Michigan to check on her. It had taken months of negotiations for her to move across country on her own. Cherise refused to lose any ground. "Everything's fine. I haven't had an attack in sixteen months. Stop worrying."

Her senior year of college had been brutal. Her mom had gotten sick. Her dad divorced his second wife, her boyfriend at the time had been killed in a senseless drive-by shooting. All of those events happened so close together, she had a tough time coping with all the changes.

Then came the panic attacks. These were nothing like the ones she'd had in high school. The chest and muscle pains, inability to sleep or focus all set her on a path that took a year of her life, leaving her with meds and therapy, to recover.

"I know, and watch your tone," her mom snapped

before sighing. "I know you're grown, and the therapist feels you have whipped the attacks and learned enough coping skills to live on your own. I know all of that. But I'm your mama and I will always worry about you. It's a part of the mama's creed."

"I knooooow, but I've worried you enough. Time for you to move on with your life. Speaking of which, how's Mr. Elmore?"

"Um hmm, nice switch. I'll let it slide this time. Elmore's the same, fine and waiting for me to lower my guard, which I have no intention of doing."

"Why not? He's a nice man."

"I'm waiting for you to start dating. How'd that look for me to be out balling and my daughter locked up tight at home? They'd take away my seal of good motherhood."

"Balling? Seal of what?" Cherise laughed. Her mom was a trip.

"You heard me. Now, when you start dating, I'll start. So don't ask me anything about my personal life until you're ready to fly."

"I'm flying." Cherise hadn't meant to say anything, not yet but hearing her mom's latest excuse loosened her tongue.

"Say what?" The doubt in her mom's tone would have been funny if it wasn't so pitiable. Had it really been that long?

"I went on a date tonight, that's one of the things I was thinking about when you called."

The silence boomed.

"I guess I should've told you," Cherise said stiltedly,

trying to gauge her mama's mood.

"No, no, you don't have to do that. I was just thinking how much I really don't want to be bothered with Elmore right now. Can we renegotiate?"

Cherise laughed, relieved. "Sure, mama, you can chicken out of your date with that fine man if you want. Although you did teach me to honor my promises." She choked on her laughter and her mom's loud sigh.

"Before I call Elmore, I need details. Not that I think you'd lie, but dang, Elmore for a few hours, whew."

"Puh-lease, I know you well enough that you'd never put him in the mix if you weren't interested." She crossed her fingers hoping her mom would take the bait and follow that trail.

"Yeah, stop stalling, give me details."

She inhaled. "I met Ross at the accident last week."

"Back that up. What accident?" Her mom barked, all joking aside.

Shit, she'd forgotten to tell her parents. "I ran a red light last week and a truck from a construction company sideswiped me, totaled the car, but I'm okay, no one was hurt, I just skinned my knee," she said in a quick breath.

"And I'm just finding out about this. Why?" Her mom growled. Cherise could see her mom sitting up at her desk, her lips tight and eyes narrowed. She was so glad to be in Michigan right now.

"Honestly mama, I forgot. I had to make up a test and it took me all weekend to decide if I wanted to take him up on his offer for dinner. You know how I obsess." She lay back on her brown suede sofa and paused the movie.

Erosa Knowles- Men of 3X CONStruction
Book 1

This might take a while.

"It took you the entire weekend to decide to go on a date? What's wrong with the man?"

Grabbing the reprieve from the accident non-discussion with both hands, she breathed a sigh of relief. "Nothing's wrong with him. It's me, remember. After everything that's happened I wanted to be sure going out to dinner was what I wanted."

"Dinner? That's it?"

"Well, we went to the pool hall after and met his friends. You'd like Smoke. Dark skinned, low hair cut, nice body and killer smile."

"He sounds good. I'm glad you had a good time. Does your Smoke have another name?"

"I don't know. I could ask Ross, he'd know since they're partners."

"Ross? Who's he? Was this an internet date or something?" Her mom asked, confused.

"Okay, let me start over." Cherise laughed. "I met Ross, my date, last week like I said." No need to bring up the accident again. "Smoke is his partner."

"Oh, got it. So what's Ross like? You didn't say."

"He looks like your old partner, Brandon. Except he's much taller and waaay bigger. Oh, and he has a close-cropped beard and dark brown hair instead of blond. Actually, his eyes are hazel, not blue."

"It sounds like the only thing they might have in common is they're both white. Is that right?" Her mom's dry tone scraped her ears.

"I guess so."

"Where'd you go for dinner?"

"That's it? Nothing else to say?"

"About?"

"Ross is a white man, mama. How do you feel about that?"

Her mom laughed. A rip roaring, loud belly-shaking laugh.

"Really, ma. Really?" Cherise said dryly, looking at her nail tips while her mom tried to stop laughing.

"Sorry baby girl, but you do fixate on the strangest things." She sniffed in an obvious attempt to stop. "But what I or anyone else thinks doesn't matter. You're the one who sat at the table with him." She coughed before saying in a more sober tone, "How'd you feel sitting across from your white date? Did you think of him as a white guy or just a man you were having a good time with?"

The question brought Cherise up short. "I had fun with him. He's smart and listens well. Not once did I feel nervous or out of my element. It's just—"

"What? It's just what?" Her mom pressed.

"He's really nice looking. He has the kind of body you see on those book covers and a boatload of confidence. I still don't understand why he wanted to spend time with me. You should have seen the women checking him out at the restaurant and the pool hall. One of them even walked up and talked to him with me standing there." Her eyes narrowed and her fingers curled into a fist.

"What'd he do?"

"What?" She'd missed her mom's comments.

Erosa Knowles- Men of 3X CONStruction
Book 1

"I asked, what'd he do when the woman approached him."

"Oh, he didn't talk to her. I think he turned his back, kept talking to his friends and me. She walked away red-faced." That memory made up for the previous one. He was streetwise and returned contempt for the disrespect served. None of his partners gave the woman a second glance either.

"Sounds good. I wouldn't worry about being able to keep his attention, and I know that's what you're hinting at. Relax, have fun. This doesn't have to be forever. It's okay that it's for right now. Don't blow it up or boil it down, okay?"

Easy for you to say. "That's what I planned to do." She tried to sound fly and flip. "He's fine and all that, but I'm just getting my feet back under me. I'll play it by ear."

"Hmmm, I'll take you at your word. Just don't analyze everything to death."

"That's more difficult, but I'm trying." A major hurdle, actually. Anthills became speed bumps; speed bumps became roadblocks, and then mountains. Mountains simply shut her down. Currently, the fine art of letting things go was as rough as her graduate level psyche class.

"You'll handle him. When do you plan to see him again?"

"I don't know. We didn't make any more plans. Tonight was probably just to see if I'd make a booty call or something. You know how that works." Her heart stuttered as she spoke. A keen sense of loss and dread pierced her at the thought of not talking to him again. For the first time in years, she had felt desirable. A good-looking man wanted her, of course, he didn't really know about her baggage, but it felt great being the center of his attention.

"Actually, I don't know how that works. Enlighten me, since you are so well versed." Her mom had turned on her courtroom voice.

Cherise cringed.

When her mom, Attorney Veronique Walters, entered the courtroom, her street-smart reputation and panache sent opposing counsel scurrying to back rooms to cut deals, quick. She and her mom weren't in the same league and that tone spelled a verbal beat down. Time to back it up.

"I'm just talking. I thought we had a good time, but he didn't ask to see me again. And you know I'm too scared to ask. Sorry about the booty call remark." She twined her fingers hoping her mom would give her another pass.

"Cherise."

Oh hell, her mom rarely used her first name. Something about her dad giving her that name.

"You have to stop being so hard on yourself, I mean it. So what if he never calls you again? That does *not* define who you are. You are a beautiful woman with a lot to offer any man. Never sell yourself short, you are not and never will be a booty call. Got that?"

"Yes, ma'am." Contrite, she rolled over and sat up.

"Now get some rest, tomorrow's another day to

Erosa Knowles- Men of 3X CONStruction
Book 1

conquer."

"Yes, ma'am."

Chapter 6

It turned out Ross was just as apprehensive as Cherise, and called two days after their dinner date to talk. In the past two weeks, the two of them spent as much of their free time together as possible getting to know each other better.

He wasn't an easy man. His mood swings worked her nerves at times. And he rarely spoke about himself, not that she blamed him. With all her baggage, she veered to the extreme left to avoid any slip-ups. After all what could she say? "By the way, my therapist just released me from a year of meds and treatment." That'd make MSNBC's "how to run away a man in one minute," list.

Cherise sat on the side of the court watching Ross, Smoke and Red play a game of pick-up basketball at the park. The moment Ross and his partner's feet hit the court, all laughing and fooling around ceased. Aliens took over. Their personalities switched that fast. In an orchestrated move, Ross and Red sent the ball to Smoke who jumped up and slammed the ball into the goal. That set the tone and pace of the game.

They were ruthless. A couple of brutal fouls made her cringe. To her surprise, Ross ignored each one on his way to complete the play. For a moment, she thought a fight would break out with a few of the other players. However, the look on Ross's face, and the attitude Red and Smoke threw out, kept everyone in check. They didn't take any attitude off the other guys and eventually won the game.

No one could explain to her how such a rough sport offered the relaxation they claimed. The moment the game was over; they slapped hands or bumped each other and headed for their trucks. The entire time their heads swiveled in all directions. Ross explained to her later they had been checking the area for possible trouble.

Where the hell had Ross grown up that he was comfortable playing ball in this type neighborhood? She'd been in school here for over a year and had never visited this section of town. Peeking over her shoulder, she noticed they were getting glances from some of the females who'd walked over and watched the game. Strange, last night at the pool hall, Red talked to anything that looked like a female. Today, he merely nodded and kept moving.

"Where'd you guys learn to play ball like that?" she asked Ross, curious of his background.

He started the truck. "We've been playing together for the last ten years. Every once and a while we find a court and play to unwind, stay focused. You play?"

"What? Basketball?"

He nodded, and pulled out behind Smoke.

"No. And that didn't look like any basketball game I've ever seen either."

"Street ball's a l'il different. Not much rules."

"It seemed rough. I had no idea it could be so brutal. Was Red hurt when that guy knocked him down?"

Ross laughed. A big heartfelt sound that echoed inside the cabin and lit a spark in her. "Just his pride. I know you expected him to take the muthafu--, chump out right?"

She smiled at his attempt to clean up his language. "Yeah, I did. Red was twice that guy's size. But, you knocked the guy down later and he didn't return to the court. Is that how y'all play? Mess with one, mess with all kind of thing."

He was silent for a moment and then glanced at her. "Yep."

Good Lord, he was so out of her league. No one in their right mind would want to tangle with all three of them. They were huge to start with. Smoke was the shortest at around six feet or an inch over. Red hit six five and Ross was slightly below that. Besides, the signals they sent clearly said *don't even think about messing with us*.

Tired, she exhaled, and looked out the window. Sleep escaped her last night, she'd thought about him. There were times she hated her analytically obsessive mind, but this man was complicated. The more time they spent together, the stronger and weaker she became.

Stronger in that her sense of self reemerged. She hadn't laughed, and enjoyed herself without fear in a long time. With him, she felt safe. Safe to argue various viewpoints, safe to sit in public places, safe to be herself.

Safety came at a price. Concealing her disorder made her weaker. The reality that her new security was built on the sands of deceit, through omission, undermined her recovery. The more she enjoyed him, the larger the fear of his rejection grew; and what that loss would do to her peace of mind.

Erosa Knowles- Men of 3X CONStruction
Book 1

"What are you thinking about? Why're you so quiet?"

"Just wondering about some stuff, that's all."

"Stuff like?"

"Where are you from?"

"You're wondering where I'm from? That's got you all quiet and looking away from me?" Disbelief filled his voice.

"Among other things, but let's start with that."

"Detroit."

"Your family still there?'

"Could be, I haven't talked to my parents in seven years." His curt tone caught her off guard.

She glanced at his tightened knuckles on the steering wheel and changed the subject. "Have you ever been married?"

"Never married, you?"

"No, I'm only 25. I've been close, but it fell apart. But I still believe in marriage. You?"

"No, not really. I've never seen a good marriage and just so you know, I don't think that's in my future." He glanced at her.

"Well, just so you know." She swallowed. "I definitely plan on getting married and having kids one day. I intend to teach and work with kids. It's something I've always wanted to do."

"I can see that." He nodded. "I think you'd be a great mom." He paused. "Where are your parents?"

Leaning back against the headrest, she sighed. "Mom is in Colorado and my dad lives in North Carolina. Military."

"Brothers? Sisters?"

"My dad has two boys with his second wife. My mom only had me. I remember wishing for a sister and asked my mom for one." She smiled in remembrance at the look of horror on her mom's face.

"What'd she say?"

"To be polite, I'll just say she said no, in colorful terms."

"Hmmm." He chuckled.

"You said you've been playing ball together and in business with Red and Smoke for a while. What made you decide to build homes?"

"I got into some trouble as a teenager. One of my counselors took me to a construction site. He said I needed to learn to do other things with my hands. He took me once every week until the house was completed. I thought it was magic. There was all this wood and shit everywhere. In the end, it turned into something beautiful. I asked a lot of questions, worked on the sites, took classes and finally started my own company."

"What's your favorite part when you build a house?"

"Hmmm, that's difficult to answer. I love the electrical and mechanical components. But brick and mortar are cool too. I think it's easier to say what I don't like that much. That would be landscaping, and maybe tile work."

Obviously, he loved his job and from what he'd said so far, he was good at it. "Have you ever built a house by yourself? I mean from start to finish?" She'd turned in the seat and faced him, enjoying the conversation. For the most part, he picked and chose what he'd answer for her. His life definitely wasn't an open book, but then neither was hers.

"Naw, not yet. That's a big deal and for the most part, I'd need help. Even if it was to hold something in place for nailing or pipefitting. I believe in working smart." He smiled. A real one that reached his eyes, before he winked at her.

She melted right there in the seat into a pile of goo. Her nipples tightened in attention as moisture flooded her panties. She squeezed her thighs close together to ease the ache, but that only made it worse. Hopefully, he missed her body's reaction as they turned into the parking lot of the extended stay hotel where he stayed.

"I'm going to get cleaned up and then we can go out for a bite. Is there something else you want to do after that? A movie, jazz club, off the chain sex?" He wiggled his brow on the last comment.

They hadn't crossed that bridge yet, but he had let her know, through touch and words, he wanted her. Today, she was primed.

"I'm not sure. Let's play it by ear." Her body throbbed in places that had been dormant for years. The ache between her legs demanded satisfaction, her womb spasmed in outrage at her denial.

You want different things in life, children, and marriage.

Her mind tried reasoning with her, but her body viciously over-ruled every argument in favor of getting horizontal with this man. For some reason, he calmed her. Maybe the fact that very little bothered him, or the manner in which he handled life's challenges. Whatever the reason she let her guard down a smidge.

Her mental white flag rose as she changed clothes in his bathroom. One night, she compromised. She'd see how she'd handle flesh-to-flesh contact. The last time she'd tried being intimate, she had a mild panic attack. Of course, she hadn't been ready. There was no easy banter or gentle touches like with Ross. Her body burned for him. She'd do one night, just this once and pray it'd be enough.

They settled on a small club with a live band and dancing after dinner. The lead singer crooned Anita Baker as swerving bodies littered the dance floor. They sat at a small two seater table near the front.

"I think I know her," she whispered to Ross. He sat with his arm casually thrown over the back of her chair, tapping his foot to the beat of the music.

"Yeah?"

"I think so, but I'm not sure. There aren't that many blacks on campus, but I may have seen *her* walking around." She took a sip of wine and listened as the woman belted out "Sweet Love."

"She's good."

"Dance with me," he said pulling her hand and leading her to the crowded floor.

"Uh, okay." Her nerves jangled as she walked in front of the small crowd. The deafening sound of swarming bees muted as she kept her eyes on his hand holding hers, warm and safe. A dull roar rose briefly but fled under her calm.

She wanted to shout her happiness; she'd slayed the beast that shadowed her for years. She inhaled. The myriad of smells in the small room almost obscured his fragrant cologne. In gratitude she looked up and smiled. He'd done this for her, helped her step beyond her comfort zone. Her mom would cry happily if she saw her right now with her arms locked around a man in front of a crowd, breathing normally.

It never occurred to her that they'd dance. From what she'd heard and seen, most white men had two left feet and simply rocked side to side. Once again, he'd surprised her. First basketball and now this.

When he wrapped his arms around her, she forgot everything. Ross pulled her close and moved in and out with the beat of the song. If she didn't know better, she'd swear they were slow-dragging, or bumping and grinding, black folk style. She couldn't help but follow his sensuous lead.

His chin dropped to the top of her head. Beneath the cologne, she caught a whiff of his natural fragrance. He smelled so good. For the first time in years, she wanted to touch another person's flesh. She buried her nose beneath the column of his throat where his shirt was unbuttoned.

"Watch it; don't start nothing up in here."

His hands tightened around her waist, the deep sexiness of his voice triggered a tightening in her nipples. Her womb clenched and her panties dampened further. She'd been on edge most of the night. He'd teased her at dinner, laughing and stroking her arms. Encased in the strength of his arms, surrounded by his heady scent, her body burned. She was on auto-pilot in search of release, from him.

"What? What're you talking about?" Was that her voice, so deep and needy?

He missed a step and pulled her closer. "Behave, or I'll snatch you right here on this floor." His voice strained. His hands palmed her ass, pulling her closer to his rock hard cock.

"Show me," she teased while grinding her woman's core on his hardened flesh.

He groaned as she rubbed her mound over him, again. He never missed a beat. Good thing the club was dark, they were playing with fire and she knew it. Reveled in it. One of them had to be the adult and stop this.

Not me, not tonight.

She bit his chest and then licked the spot. He stopped moving, turned her around and marched them back to their table. She thought they were going to sit down, but he grabbed his jacket from the back of the chair and pulled her behind him out the door.

"Hold up," she said, pulling back. "My shoe is coming off." She snatched her hand from him and fixed her shoe. The cool air returned her sanity and cooled her ardor.

Not so with her date.

A red tint crept up his neck and stained his tight face. Even in the night, she could tell his eyes weren't their normal light brown. He frowned when he realized she'd finished with her shoe and stared at him.

He grabbed her hand and steered her towards the truck.

"Ross — "

"Not a word Cherise, not another damn word."

Surprised, she stepped up into the truck and fastened her seat belt. Glancing at his profile, she noticed his clenched jaw and pinched lips. Turning away, she looked out the window and smiled. He'd lost his cool. She'd bet the farm that didn't happen often.

"Are you mad at me?" she asked, trying to sound timid.

Not fooled, he glared at her. "No, not at all. Why should I be?" His soft words were at odds with his tense posture.

"You snapped at me. I thought you were mad." It took a year of therapy for her to engage in this type of light teasing. No panic, no anxiety, no fear. She fully intended to ride this train tonight. Tomorrow was a different day.

He sighed. "Cherise, I wanted to give you what I thought you wanted, needed. Dinner, dancing, whatever. I did that for *you*. Me, I would tie you down to my bed and just have room service. If we are going to have sex, and we are—" He sent her a hard stare. "—you cannot play with me like that in public. I know you don't know me that well, but for real, you can't be doing that shit. I *will* respond. I felt like pulling your legs up on the dance floor and sexing you every way 'til Sunday. And that's real."

Her mouth dropped open. She waited for the panic flare up. Nothing, nada. Calm flowed over her heating her core. She could enjoy this.

"So you're saying you only went out tonight because I wanted to, but you would have rather been in bed screwing my brains out. And you can rub on my ass, smell and taste like sin, but I can't respond to you, because *you* can't handle it." She smirked at his frown.

"I don't like how it sounds when you put it like that, but yeah, that's about right."

"Hmmm."

Ross smoothed his face and hair with his palm. Thank God tomorrow was Sunday, he hoped she didn't have plans, because he wouldn't be letting her go until late. He moved in the seat, trying to get comfortable.

Impossible.

He needed to be inside her, stat. He glanced at her biting her lower lip. Huh-uh, now she worries. She'd been teasing him all night, touching his hand, leaning on his chest, grinding on his cock. He'd almost exploded on the floor.

Pissed him off, it'd been years since he lost control like that. Hell, it'd been years since he felt like this about anyone. Edgy, excited and concerned at the same time. It didn't make sense. She talked a lot, analyzed everything, tried to tell him how he felt, he should leave her ass alone, but he'd never wanted anyone more.

Cherise called to a part of him he didn't know existed. After spending the past two weeks and today with her, he wanted that woman with a bone deep hunger that surpassed anything he'd ever felt. When she listened to him talk, he wanted to beat his chest at the light of interest in her eyes. Ready or not, he was in. If calling it a relationship was what it'd take to keep that sparkle in her eyes for him, so be it.

"Come on." He jumped out and headed for his suite. He stopped and turned. "What the hell?" he murmured. She sat in the truck looking at him. Returning to the truck, he opened her door and held a hand to assist her down.

"Sorry about that," he mumbled.

"You should be. Never forget, Ross, treat me with respect at all times, no matter what's going down." They stared at one another a second.

The realization of how serious she was slapped him dead center. He should've known better, he couldn't let his little head get in the way of treating her right. Although she'd never demanded anything specific from him, respect should be a given and worked both ways.

He nodded. "Got it." Taking her hand, he walked them towards his unit.

"You want something to drink?" he asked locking the door behind them.

"No."

"You're not changing your mind about— anything, are you?" He prayed she wasn't a teaser.

"No, I just don't need anything to drink, that's all." She moved to the sofa and kicked off her shoes. Bending from her waist, she leaned down and picked them up. "Where can I put — these?"

He grabbed her hand, and dragged her to the open door, next to the dining area. "Here, everything you need will be in here." He smacked her butt as she sashayed past him.

She gasped and paused. "Ow, hey, no hitting!" She rubbed her posterior and glared at him.

"Come here, let me kiss it and make it all better." He couldn't help it. She'd deliberately taunted him when she stuck her ass in the air picking up those shoes. He'd warned her not to play with him. He moved towards her, his intent evident.

She backed away, smiling.

The little imp wanted to play; he'd try, but was nearing the end of his patience. He stopped. Two could play this game. He unbuckled his belt.

Her entire demeanor changed as he drew his belt out and dropped it to the floor. Next, he unsnapped his pants and zipped them down. Her eyes were glued to the movements of his hands. His cock rose higher in appreciation of the glaze of lust that flashed in her eyes as he rolled his pants down. He threw his shirt on the floor.

Her breath caught.

He smiled as she licked her lips while he palmed his heavy cock through his boxers, granting her hungry eyes a peek of the mushroomed tip every once and a while. He pushed them down and stroked his bare penis.

"Take off your dress." He said while rolling on a condom.

She nodded and pulled the straps down exposing her bare breasts, which stood at attention. The material caught at her hips, she shimmied, causing it to fall to the floor. Her index finger grabbed her thong, and it followed the dress.

Erosa Knowles- Men of 3X CONStruction
Book 1

Truthfully, he couldn't process a thought. Her full breasts stood at attention while her raisin colored peaks pebbled at his inspection.

He swallowed hard.

Dry mouthed, his eyes traveled over her luscious brown form, pass the ring piercing her naval, down to her neatly trimmed, glistening vee. Instinct owned him; he had to make her his, now.

He moved forward, picked her up and dropped her on the bed. Her breast flattened against his chest as his mouth attacked her lips, neck and then her breasts. The need to brand her overrode his game plan and common sense. Beneath the light perfume and the shea butter was her unique smell. His nose rubbed her neck, seeking to get closer, to smear her scent on him.

She pulled him tighter, kissing his face, stroking his skin, fanning the flames of his hunger for her.

"Next time, next time I'll be slow. Right now I can't." That was the extent of his warning before he slammed into her.

"So tight, so good," he moaned as he pulled out and slammed forward again.

"Awwww," Cherise groaned.

He stopped. *Please God, no.* "Are you okay?" he whispered, trying to reign in his lust.

A slap on his backside was the answer. "Move!"

"Hell, yeah." He started stroking her again. Her legs tightened around his waist. He pulled them higher to go deeper. His thrusts pulled him closer to the edge, the walls of her tunnel tightened around him. His back arched as he pounded home

"Ohmigod, ohmigod," she screamed.

He thrust faster, pulled her legs higher. "So close, close" he huffed.

He felt her tense, and then shudder beneath him, milking him as he exploded.

Chapter 7

Cherise returned home intending to get some rest before retaking her exam this afternoon. Neither she nor Ross got much sleep last night. He'd been insatiable. So had she for that matter. She celebrated her freedom to touch, fuss and be herself by indulging in sexy pleasing games.

First thing on her list was a hot, soak in the tub, to ease some of the pain from her sensitive folds and thighs. Later, she lay face down on her bed, drifting to sleep when one of her new ring tones, James Brown yelled, "I feel good," announcing she had a call.

"What?" She grouched into the phone. Talking was the last thing on her mind.

"Tsk, tsk, that's no way to answer the phone. I called to check up on you. Haven't heard from you in a while."

Cherise groaned. God must be angry with her. "Jackie, I'm sleepy. I got an exam at three this afternoon and I don't feel up to you right now. Talk to you later."

"Wait! Don't hang up. Damn, you are definitely Veronique's child. You sound just like her. I need to talk to you." She paused. "It's important."

"What?" Cherise knew she sounded ungracious. But the woman pissed her off, always thinking what she wanted was more important than anything else. Besides, they weren't close, not by a long shot. There was no reason to be polite.

"Meow, somebody's in a catty mood." Jackie twittered at her own wit.

Cherise growled.

"Okay, okay, I'll be brief. I'm getting married in a few months and I want *you* to be my maid of honor."

Thanks, but no thanks. "I'm sorry, I can't do that." Cherise continued in the silence on the line. "I'm finishing up my degree in a few months and then I'll be starting at my new job. I won't be able to get away. Thanks for thinking about me, though." She added the last bit as an afterthought.

"I can't accept no for an answer. You have to be my maid of honor. You're my cousin."

"Not any longer, your Aunt divorced my dad. Remember." Finally, she could throw the disconnection in the heifer's face. Her people only claimed kinship when they thought it'd benefit them. "Besides, your family has never accepted me or my mom and I'm not down with anyone dissing her." She yawned. "Like I said, I'm tired and need some sleep." If she had the energy, she'd applaud her therapist and all the training she'd received the past year. Standing up for herself rocked.

"Please."

"Jackie, I said no. Stop pushing me. Get one of your girlfriends to do the honors." She clicked off. Within seconds, James Brown bellowed again. Her phone was the only thing in the room feeling good.

Cherise snatched the pillow from off her head. "Don't do this, I'm trying to be nice," she growled into the phone.

"I don't have a choice, Cherise." The voice sounded small and pathetic. "The wedding is in ten weeks and I don't have a wedding party. No maid of honor, no bridesmaids. Bruce has all his guys lined up." She said the words fast. Gone was the teasing and condescending tone. Desperation had stepped to the forefront and waved its flag.

"Where are all those friends you bragged to me about last year?" Cherise rolled over, pulling the pillow over her eyes.

"They can't do it either. It'll just be you. Please Cherise, please."

She sighed, hating she wasn't as strong as her mom. Veronique wouldn't have answered the call if she knew it was someone she didn't want to talk to. Their family had coined the term, 'Veroniqued' in her mom's honor for feisty comebacks and remarks.

"I don't have any money for a wedding." She hoped this would be the deal breaker; Jackie had a reputation for being tight-fisted, like a big woman in a girdle a size too small.

"That's all right," she said brightly. "I'll cover everything. Just tell me your size and I'll order it."

She groaned in defeat, but maid of honor! Jackie must be scraping pretty low to have asked her. They were cordial at best.

"No, ma'am. I have to see it first. No offense, but I'm not looking stupid walking down the aisle in an ugly dress, even if I don't pay for it. Send me the choices in an email. I'll pick one and send it back. Then you can order it."

"That's great. We're getting married in Lansing. I'll email you all the information. I'll need you here for the dress rehearsal and dinner. Those should be the night before. I'll check with the planner."

"Uh-huh." She'd started to drift off again.

"Will you be bringing a date?"

"What?" Her mind struggled to keep up with the conversation.

"A date, companion, someone to be with. Preferably a man."

"I dunno, just met a guy, might bring him." She rolled over, punched the pillow in the middle and laid her head down.

"Ohhhhh," Jackie squealed. "You got a boyfriend? What does he do?"

Cherise pulled the phone away from her ears and then returned it. She hated the perky voice. "Of course, the first thing you want to know is what he does. And I never said I had a boyfriend."

"Hey, we're family — okay, almost family. Gotta look out for each other."

"Notice, I haven't asked what your fiancé does, nor have I asked any personal questions about him. Why? Because it's none of my business. I respect your privacy. Respect mine."

"But you can ask," she whined, obviously itching to brag on her future husband. "I don't mind talking about Bruce."

"I mind! I'm tired and you've already gotten what you want from me. Don't call me back. I'm not going to answer." She yawned and clicked off. James Brown yelled again, she sent him to voice mail.

Erosa Knowles- Men of 3X CONStruction
Book 1

###

"Ross, I need you to sign those contracts and get them back to me as soon as possible. The next job starts in about three and a half months. Will that enough time to finish up there and take a break? Or do you need more time?" Connie, the sixty-one-year-old office manager, asked.

"Yeah, should be good. We should be doing a final here in six weeks, give or take a few days. Send the contracts overnight and I'll get them back to you. Have the new guys reported in?"

"Yes, Julio Cardenas and Theodore Beckins had their physicals, which came back clean."

"Good, I told them, no drugs. I wasn't sure about Theo, but I'm glad he's clean. The man has the best touch with any type of stone and is an artist with brick. I'd have hated to lose him."

Theo was an egomaniac, of small stature. Prison hadn't been that kind to him. By the time he entered the construction program, he'd been mentally and physically abused. Ross only agreed to offer him the job as a favor to Rubie, his mentor. He'd been tough when he interviewed the man, laying everything on the line.

Theo explained he had a wife and two kids. His wife had waited while he was in prison and would be relocating to the area whenever he found work, they'd come to an understanding. Coupled with a warning that if Theo tried to fuck over their company, what he experienced in prison would be child's play. The three of them had tough enough reputations to back up the promise. Theo knew it as well.

"What's Julio's specialty? He didn't say much. When I took them through orientation and set them up with the banker to open their accounts for payroll, he didn't blink. Had no questions. Even Theo had questions about the starting salary and vacation times. But that one, Julio, simply signed everything without batting an eye." Connie was always curious of the workers and their habits. As long as she stayed out of their personal business, it was fine. He hoped her curiosity didn't have her crossing the line. He'd hate to lose her.

"How much are you starting them at?" He asked instead of answering her question.

"Fifteen dollars an hour for the first ninety days on automatic deposits twice a month, scheduled to go up after that. I went with the standard rates. Is that all right? Should I change it for them?" By keeping the majority of the trades in-house, they were able to pay decent stable wages. The company paid salaries instead of hourly and automatic deposits since they had so many out of town jobs.

"No, that's a good start. I thought Smoke may have said something. Never mind. Julio is a master with cabinetry and trim work. Some of the custom work he's created will make you drool. He's that good. A little on the quiet side, but very talented. I'm surprised Smoke was able to talk him into coming this way."

Julio in the mix would be interesting. Smoke and the man had some history. He hadn't been in the places the others had; he'd gone straight into training from juvie, spending the rest of his time there. The stories they'd told him made him grateful for the training and the opportunity to turn his life around. Prison was no Disneyland.

"How's Doug?" Her husband had apprenticed him and was suffering with an illness.

"Probably best as can be expected. The hospice nurse keeps him comfortable. It's hard seeing him slip away like this. He heard the pain in her voice for her husband of forty some years. "Rubie came to see him the other day."

"That's good. He cancelled dinner the other night; I need to get up with him about some things."

"I hired a lovely Latina to help in the office. I needed some back up, especially since I plan on cutting back my hours to spend more time with Doug."

"Sure, no problem." He answered looking at some papers she'd sent a few days before. Absently, he went over the finances. They'd come in under budget with this project, profit margins were higher than projected.

"Okay, who is she, Ross? Ross!"

"Huh?"

"I asked, who is she?"

"Who's who?" he asked, not following the conversation.

"I just informed you that I hired a lovely Latina woman and you asked no questions. Now we both know that's unheard of. I had my 'leave the girl alone' speech all ready and you don't even nibble. That means you're already pre-occupied, so tell me, who is she?"

Damn, he'd forgotten Ms. Connie was sharp as a tack. A new woman at the office? They'd promised Rubie his niece could work there. He'd check to see if she was still interested.

"You know, I could say you're wrong."

"You could, but you don't lie to me," she fired back. "Not much anyway."

"Aw, now that's wrong. I'm pretty straight up with you. You're like a mom to me."

"Um, hmmm. Stop stalling, who you taking up with?"

He placed the papers to the side and closed his eyes, seeing Cherise's face, her smile, hearing her laugh at something he or one of the guys said. "Her name's Cherise. I met her six weeks ago. We've been talking and seeing each other since then." He paused. "She's cool."

"Hmmm. She the only one you seeing right now?"

"Yep, we hardly see each other, though. She's in school."

"School? How old is this child?"

He smiled at the reprimand in her voice. If only she knew. There was nothing childish about Cherise's mind or body. Her upbringing was nothing like his. From the bits and pieces he gathered, her mom was a hoot and spared no punches preparing her daughter for the real world.

"Twenty-five, she's working on her Masters' in Education, I believe."

"Oh my, an educated woman? What's she going to teach?"

"Huh?"

"Is she going to teach, elementary, middle, administration? Which education field is she in?"

"I don't know. She did say she wanted to teach kids, though."

"Well, I'm happy for you. Bring her to the Collier fund raiser in a couple of weeks."

He groaned having forgotten all about the gala for sick kids. Connie had talked them into contributing a few years ago, and they'd been partial sponsors of the event ever since. "It depends on where we are with this project, I'm not sure I can make it." His excuse was lame, he knew it and so did she.

"Ivey Green's been calling to see when you're returning. I think she's holding out for an invite. Yep, she's had a thing for you for years."

He recoiled. "You say her full name on purpose, knowing it messes with me. Who names their child Ivey *and* green? It ain't right."

She laughed. "You better bring a date or she'll be clinging like ivy to you."

He shook his head as she laughed at his expense. He'd make sure and invite Cherise tomorrow night when they got together. No way would he chance an attachment to Ivy at any point during the fundraiser. The woman had tough skin and ignored all his rejections.

"Yeah, I'll think on it. Since I'll be coming home next weekend, I'll skip this one. I think Red and a couple of the crew will be down to exchange equipment out. Don't forget to send our mail."

"Have I ever forgotten?"

"No ma'am."

Chapter 8

Friday rolled around, clear and crisp. Ross was on his way to pick Cherise up for dinner. Between her school and his job, they had to make every time they got together count. Ever since his talk with Ms. Connie, he'd been anxious to see her. Although they talked daily, it wasn't the same as watching the way she tilted her head in interest when he spoke. Or her hot response to him when they got physical instead of just phone sex. Tonight he'd invite her to go home to Lapeer and the gala next weekend. Perhaps she could stay an extra day and they could hang out, he'd show her some sights.

He sighed in satisfaction, driving mindlessly. The construction project was on schedule and under budget. Next week they should be able to install the cabinetry and hardwood floors. They had another two- three weeks at this job and then a long winter break before they traveled to the next one. He'd taken Cherise to view the house and took immense pride in her praise of their hard work. Her real interest in his job surprised and pleased him.

For the first time he could remember, he experienced genuine admiration from a woman. It fed him. He felt taller, stronger, validated. He'd convinced himself that the sparkle he noticed in her eyes was unique and special. Meant only for him.

She met him at her door and jumped into his arms. He kissed her hard as he walked her back into the apartment. "You ready babe?" He pulled her tight against him, inhaling her peaches and vanilla scents. She smelled so good.

"Yeah," she purred, rubbing against him. He loved when she was in a playful mood. The sex would be hotter, sharper and more satisfying.

He rose at the thought and smacked her bottom. "Behave, I have to eat something besides you. Come on, let's go." He pulled her forward.

She laughed. "Slow down. I have to lock the door."

"Hurry up, the sooner we finish eating dinner, the sooner I can take care of you."

"Promises, promises," she mocked, walking beside him.

He grabbed her hand, and bit the middle of her palm. "Not a promise, a straight up guarantee." He licked and kissed the same spot, smiling at the tremor that ran through her.

They drove in companionable silence to the restaurant. He liked she didn't feel the need to talk *all* the time. Some days it was good to listen to music or news and enjoy one another. They'd been sitting for around thirty minutes, eating with some light conversation, when he felt the heavy stare of someone. He looked up and inwardly groaned when the man changed directions and made a beeline to their table.

"Hey, Ross! How are you? I heard you and the guys were building a big custom home up here. Everybody okay?" He asked, slapping Ross on the shoulder.

Ross glanced at the frown on Cherise's face. She smoothed it over and looked at Mark Kenney, his old probation officer. Swallowing down another groan, he pasted 'his glad to see ya smile' on and prepared to wade through the bullshit. *Fuck, he should have told her!*

"Everybody's good Mr. K. We're building a house not too far from here." He cut his answer short, hoping the man would move on. His mind raced. If he introduced Cherise, maybe he could play it off. An old friend or something like that.

"Let me intro—"

"Hold on, a colleague of mine was at a conference recently about prisoner training and I told him about your success story." He paused looking around the restaurant and waved over a thin, pale man to the table. The newcomer moved towards them with considerable grace considering how packed the area was.

Ross glanced at Cherise. She continued eating, her wrinkled forehead the only indication she paid attention. He could imagine how she'd analyze his not telling her.

"There he is."He waved vigorously. "Come, come, Jerry, this is one of the young men I told you about. They are building a huge house here in Big Rapids for one of the local fat cats. I heard it was over 5,000 square feet, a multi-million dollar deal. Ross came into the system early. That's one of the things they tell you in those conferences, the training works best if you catch them early before they get an ugly taste of prison life."

Ross swallowed the pungent taste of humiliation as his former parole officer talked about him as if he weren't there. As if he had every right to infringe on his personal life and time, to earn brownie points. He couldn't look at Cherise. Each word spoken reminded him of a time in his life when each day was a struggle to survive. No one wanted to give ex-cons a chance. He worked for sub-minimum pay, and on days when hardly anyone else showed up, he did. Every dirty construction job, he drew the unlucky straw. Now, this motherfucker stood here taking credit!

Oh, Hell, no!

Breathing deeply, he looked at the opposite wall, and reminded himself of a few things. You own a multi-million dollar business. People depend on you staying cool, calm. Do *not* allow this chubby sonofabitch cause you to lose it up in here. He means less than crap to you.

"The training is good for a lot of the guys. I was lucky, *my instructor* knew a few people who gave me a break." Ross turned, refusing to look at either man, his voice strong despite the raging anger in the pit of his stomach.

"Yes, yes, that's right. That's an important part of the training. Convicts need a stable environment when they leave. Having trainers or someone in admin who can connect them to the construction industry is the best way to keep them from returning to prison. Ross and his friends are a tremendous success for the program. We hope to mimic those results repeatedly in the future." The man's florid cheeks, puffed out as if he'd said something new. Ross twisted his lips and turned away.

"Mr.?" the thin man asked, reaching his hand toward Ross.

"Stemple, but Ross's fine," he answered taking the man's pale hand and looking into his pale blue eyes.

"I apologize for interrupting your dinner with your

lovely companion." He nodded in Cherise's direction, and pulled a business card from his pocket. "Please, here's my card. Call me when you have some time. Building custom homes is no easy matter, and you have my utmost respect. We are considering a similar program in my area of Wisconsin." He nodded at Cherise and then Mr. K, who'd reddened at the indirect rebuke.

"I'm sorry, Ross," his ex-probation officer said before turning to Cherise. "Miss, please forgive my manners. I wasn't thinking." His face completely red now, his eyes slid from one to the other. "That was rude of me to intrude this way. Ross's no longer under my jurisdiction, but I'm proud of him. So few of the men we work with make it...well, sorry," he mumbled and followed his colleague.

A heavy silence descended on the table. Cherise picked up her glass and drank her tea. Ross watched as she stared at the other tables, and ate mechanically. Picking up his fork, he continued eating.

"Well, that was awkward," Cherise muttered.

"Yeah." He stared at his plate, afraid to look up and see her reaction to the news. His fingers played with the edge of the business card.

"You gonna call him?'

"Probably."

"Excuse me." She rose and walked from the table.

He watched as she asked a waiter a question, nodded and headed towards the restrooms. Exhaling, he threw his cloth napkin on the table and placed the card in his pocket.

"Damn Mark and his big mouth." Even as he voiced it, he knew he should've told her himself. But hell, what was he supposed to say. *I'm an ex-con. Let's go to dinner, dancing and then get busy.*

He shook his head. Experience had taught him that the kind of women turned on by his short stint in prison, were not the type he'd trust very far. And while he didn't believe in a happily ever after, he did want a happy for now.

Okay, so now she knew. The question was how to play it from here. His fingers tapped the table as he sorted through his mental repertoire. The waiter removed his plate. Games wouldn't work with Cherise. The risk of a walkout and no sex was too high. He'd just have to tell the truth and talk her out of dropping him like yesterday's trash.

He glanced at his watch, she still hadn't returned. He'd considered sending in a waitress when she walked towards him. Sitting down, she picked up her glass and drained it with her eyes closed.

He waited for her to look at him.

She avoided his eyes and picked at her food, moving it around the plate.

"Say it, whatever's on your mind." He moved his clenched fist beneath the table and continued tapping his fingers with the other.

She shrugged. "I don't have anything to say."

He nodded. *So it's going to be like that.* "All right. Since you're playing with your food, and you've preached to me on how rude that is, are you ready to go?" He knew impatience threaded his tone. But, he'd just been disrespected in front of his woman. The knowledge he'd fucked up and should've been the one to tell her, also messed with him. Now she played damn coy.

"Actually, no, I'm not ready. I want some desert." She looked up and waved the waiter over. "I liked that brownie surprise I saw on the menu earlier. The one with the ice cream and nuts on top."

"That's one of our popular deserts, do you want whipped cream?" The waiter refilled her glass.

She grimaced. "No, no whipped cream. Thanks." When the waiter left, she picked up her glass of water and drank.

"You can't catch it, you know." He scowled down at the table where she'd pulled her hand from his.

"What?"

"You can't catch prison-*itis* or convict-*itis*. It's not a disease you pick up from touching. In fact, you have to do a crime or at least someone has to think you did a crime in order for convict to come on you." He looked up at her and wished he hadn't. Her face lacked all expression; she'd closed down on him. He couldn't read her and didn't know how to handle it. Was she angry? Disappointed?

"I know that." Her voice held no emotion, no pain, and no fury— nothing, and that scared the shit out of him.

"Do you? Then why won't you let me touch you?" he growled. Frustration and fear made him careless. "Afraid you might get dirty? I'm the same person now that I was last night and yesterday." Going on the offensive was instinctive, although not necessarily smart. He couldn't stop. He hated this dread of losing her, of not being enough because of his past.

"No one said you weren't."

He sighed; it was hard to fight when she sounded so calm. "I'm sorry, I should've told you myself."

"Why?"

"Why? Why I shoulda told you?'

"Yeah, why?" She made room for the desert the waiter placed in front of her.

He waited until the waiter left. "Because it's the honest and real thing to do," he said, hoping that's what she wanted to hear.

"If I had been to prison, would you have expected me to tell you?"

He stilled. The question caught him off guard. Would he even be interested in her if she'd been in prison? He didn't like the *hell no* bubbling up within him and tamped it down. He watched her eat the brownie concoction as he thought about her question. How *would* he feel if she'd kept that from him? Tricked? Angry? He wasn't sure of which emotion, but he wouldn't like not knowing something like that. He paused at her half smile. *Naw, he would've known, wouldn't he?*

"Quit playing. I would've known if you'd spent time in the cage. No need to tell me."

"For real? How? You think because I'm in college now, I couldn't have been in prison before? Turned my life around?"

Like you did was implied, though left unsaid.

"I think it's different with women prisoners. Prison changes them, makes them hard— "He stopped at her stare and arched brow.

"All right, true, it affects some men the same way." He admitted under her disbelieving stare. This was one of those rare times he wished she wasn't so smart.

"So, if I had been to prison you would want me to tell you, right?"

"Yeah." He didn't like the double standard. *Hell how'd she back him up like this?*

"And the reason you would want to know is so you can choose if you wanted to deal with someone who might be hardened by the experience." Her eyes caught his.

He couldn't lie, it may cost him, but he wouldn't. He nodded.

"So, I'll ask you again, why are you apologizing to me?"

"Damn it, Cherise, I already told you. I thought it was what you wanted. What more do you want me to say?" He hadn't meant to raise his voice, but fear warred with aggravation, pride and a whole lot of man stuff inside.

"Obviously not much," she snapped. Fire flashed in her eyes. "If we can't have a civil conversation. But let me tell you this right now. I've *never* disrespected you and I'll be damned if I allow you to dis me. You don't raise your voice at me when I ask you a question. And heads up, apologizing cause you think it's what I wanna hear don't mean shit. So kiss my ass!" Her voice rose to a shout towards the end. She stood, snatched her purse, and headed for the door.

Oh shit, she's leaving. Ross jumped up and caught

her arm, ignoring the interested looks patrons sent their way. He couldn't let her leave like this. She tugged, he held fast. Glancing at the table, he peeled off a large bill, threw it down, and then followed her outside. He needed her to calm down. All week he'd been waiting to spend this weekend with her.

"Cherise, can we talk before you run off?" He strove to be calm, placating.

She turned and looked at him, arms crossed and head tilted with narrowed eyes, daring him to say the wrong thing.

"I'm sorry. I admit I'm not good at this. A lot of shit happened tonight. You're right; we can have a real convo." He pulled his hand through his hair and looked down at her. She looked around the parking lot, knowing that annoyed him.

He gritted his teeth. "I shouldn't have raised my voice. Ask me anything you want to know."

"It doesn't matter. I have to get home anyway. I have a long day tomorrow." She moved to pass him. He touched her arm, delaying her.

"What do you mean *you* have a long day tomorrow? I thought we were spending it together?" His chest tightened. He hadn't expected her to turn from him because of his past or maybe he did and that's why he hid it from her. Either way, he wasn't ready for her to walk out of his life.

"I'm going to Lansing to meet with Jackie."

"Jackie?"

"Yeah, my dad's ex's-niece."

"How come you never mentioned this trip?" He

narrowed his eyes at her.

She straightened, eyeing him up and down. "Ross, I don't tell you everything, and obviously you don't tell me everything. When you picked me up, I didn't have an overnight bag like last weekend, did I?" She turned and walked off towards the truck.

Visions of a long, passion-filled weekend fizzled before his eyes and belched in a stream of smoke. Reaching the truck, she waited. He caught up, unlocked the door and assisted her inside. Everything fell apart. He didn't know how to fix it, or rewind time.

"Cherise, I should've told you I'm an ex-con. In a reversed situation, true—I wouldn't handle finding out like this well either. My only excuse is, I thought you wouldn't want to be with me if you knew. I realized after our first date that you weren't the kind of person who'd hold a person's past against them. But," he shrugged, "old habits die hard. I fucked up. I was mad, not at you or even foul ass Mr. K. That's still no excuse for raising my voice at you and you had every reason to cuss me out in front of everyone in the restaurant."

He caught a glimmer of her smile, although he'd never admit it to her, she was sexy as hell in a rage. "I planned on spending the week-end with you. Even though we don't run everything by each other, you knew I thought we'd be together. So I have to wonder why you didn't tell me about your trip until after you discovered my ex-convict status."

She shrugged and looked out the window.

"You know I don't like it when you do that."

Erosa Knowles- Men of 3X CONStruction
Book 1

"Not my problem."

"What's not your problem?"

"Your likes and dislikes, not my problem. Are you going to start the truck? I wanna go home now."

He stared at the back of her head and tried to understand. He'd apologized and explained. What else could he do? Beg?

Hell no.

Fuck it. He was done.

He started the truck and spun out of the parking lot, his teeth ground in frustration. Within minutes, they arrived at her apartment complex. He sat staring forward. Damned if he'd open the door for her.

After a second's hesitation, he snatched open his door, strode to the other side and opened her door. She stepped down without touching him, picked up her purse and headed towards her unit. He slammed the door, walked to his side and pulled off.

Cherise slammed her apartment door and threw her purse on the sofa. "Ewww," she screamed in frustration.

He made her so mad. Why couldn't he talk to her? A complete stranger walks up and talks about his life in prison. Prison! They'd been seeing each other for over a month and he never mentioned something so significant. It would explain his reluctance in getting too close. It sure as hell explained the thugs that were his partners. They were cool with her and good at what they did, but she didn't doubt for a moment that they could flip it in a minute.

Sighing she dropped onto the sofa and stared at the ceiling. He'd been so cool, so unconcerned at her response, she couldn't handle it. She'd gone into the restroom and sat in a stall with her head in her hands. Her mind went into a tailspin of all the possibilities, things he could've done. People change and he probably had. But could she be with a rapist? Murderer? Pedophile? Drug Lord? Oh God! Her stomach roiled.

"Please, please, please God, let it be something small, like stealing. No! Not that. Um — I don't know what, but no blood, no children and no old people."

The hairline crack in the wall of her confidence scared her. He'd been too good to be true, she castigated herself. Good looking, hard working, single and straight— she should've guessed something was wrong somewhere.

"What the hell did you do, Ross?" She whispered.

Jumping up, she glanced at the packed suitcase, near the door. She'd already packed her laptop, so she turned on the desktop computer. Wiping her face, she clicked the keys. She'd planned to ask Ross to go with her to Lansing after dinner. She figured after she tried on the dress for the wedding tomorrow, they'd be free to hang out and check out the town together. The hotel room was booked for later tonight.

Change of plans. She needed to think this through. Online she reserved a car, moved some money around, and went to the Offender Tracking Information System to pull up information on him.

She typed in his information. No response. Damn, they only listed inmates for three years after they left the system. He'd been gone longer than that. There was one

Erosa Knowles- Men of 3X CONStruction
Book 1

person who'd definitely look into it and find out what he did. She'd contact her mom later.

Of course, it would be better if he told her, if they were to have any type of future. *Future*, she grimaced. Before the word tasted like roses and sweets, now it rolled over her tongue like sawdust. He would be leaving in a few weeks after they finished the house. She'd be graduating in four and she still hadn't decided which job she'd take.

One thing for certain, she'd be leaving Big Rapids, although not Michigan. They hadn't talked about seeing each other pass those events.

She missed him already. She needed to be strong. She needed to talk to her mama.

Chapter 9

Ross's forehead rested against the metal doorframe of Cherise's apartment. Injured pride and male ego bullshit had him driving off in a pique. After letting her out the truck, he'd made it two blocks before turning around. He parked and sat in her lot like a lovesick pup for a few minutes debating how to go forward.

Slowly, he raised his fist and knocked. He waited, thumbs in his back pockets. The night was cool and perfect for groveling. He'd come prepared to do that and more. The door opened slowly.

He exhaled. "I'm sorry. Can I talk to you?"

He walked past her as she moved back to let him in. She still wore her tailored gray pants and red silk shirt from dinner. His body reacted to her round hips and high breasts. Moisture pooled in his mouth as he walked to the middle of the living room. Perspiration dotted his brow. Nervous, he looked around the small room, trying to pull his thoughts together. He zeroed in on her suitcase and other bag.

Pushing back the sour taste of disappointment, he nodded in the direction of the luggage. "You going to Lansing?"

"Yeah." She cleared her throat. "I have that fitting tomorrow, so I have to go." Cherise walked to the counter that separated the tiny kitchen and living room.

He followed.

She turned, leaned back against the countertop and

stared at him. He took in her full lips, smooth skin, and questioning eyes. *Just tell it so you can move on.*

"I'm sorry for arguing with you. Tell me how to make this right. I don't want you mad with me. I can't lose you over my past." He reached out and took her hand. Exhaling he released pent up tension, when she didn't draw away.

"It's not over your past, Ross. I just can't believe you didn't tell me something so major." She looked up at him, waiting for something.

He released her hand and placed both his palms on the counter behind her, caging her in. "Tell me when's the right moment to tell another person your past bullshit, your damn secrets that you don't wanna face, your skeletons?" His eyes skewered hers. Everyone claimed to want to know shit, but there was a price to the telling.

"I know people who marry and never share some of their secrets," he said, inching closer. "A lot of shit dies with them. How do *you* know when it's right to share? Because I've no idea how to ride that train."

The pink tip of her tongue leisurely moistened her lips. "I think when you care about someone, you build to a level of trust and you take them into your confidence."

A level of trust, female bullshit.

"Yeah, but that's the problem. It's easier to give your body, than your deep personal history."

She ducked her head.

He continued speaking in a low whisper. "I mean the real stuff that's close to your heart. The messed up stuff everybody keeps locked up. Most folk don't get close enough to ever see the dark places inside." He watched her swallow hard.

"So I ask again, how do *you* know when's the right time." He leaned next to her ear and whispered. "After how many dinners, or dates? Before or after we have sex? What's the magic number that opens the door to my past, 'cause I damn sure ain't telling everybody my personal business."

His voice remained conversationally low, calm, while nerves jumped and pulsed at the thought of sharing some of the things he'd done in the past. He'd rather buy anything she demanded, or take her anywhere in the world, than fully open up and let her see some of the murky places in him. He didn't like to look inside and rarely did.

She narrowed her eyes. "This isn't about everybody. It's about you and me." She pushed his chest. He stepped closer.

"Okay, what signals do I get to let me know I should trust you with my baggage? You ready for that?" They looked at each other.

Her eyes slid to his chest. "I don't know."

"And therein lies the root of our problem." He dropped his arms.

She shivered.

"You want me to tell you everything without securing my trust. Why should I bare my soul to you? What would you do with the knowledge? Trust me? Or judge me?" He pulled back and stared into chocolate pools of light. Whatever this was between them marked him. He'd never considered telling a woman he dated

Erosa Knowles- Men of 3X CONStruction
Book 1

about his past. The price of admission, Red called it.

"It's like leaving pieces of your soul around and that's too damn dangerous to do on a small tip." He lifted her face with his finger.

"What have you given me? We've shared our bodies, but I know as little of you as you do of me. You haven't given me your heart or your trust. So don't leave me because of my past. My present and future are what's important." He poured his heart and soul into the words he spoke. He needed her in his life. Right now he couldn't, wouldn't process why. He just knew it with a bone deep certainty.

With deliberate movements, she pushed his chest. He stepped back, allowing her to walk to the sofa. She sat and looked over her shoulder at him.

"What did you do?" She whispered.

"I did some crazy as a teen, spent some time in juvie and then the prison build program. When I got out, I had my record expunged, set up my business and moved forward with my life."

Her eyes slid away.

"Never killed anybody." He tried to keep the exasperation from his tone. He'd bared his heart and she hadn't heard him.

"What about ra— "

His eyes narrowed, and his nostrils flared. "I know you're not thinking rape." He swallowed as a look of shame crossed her face. Damn, did she not know him at all? His hands dropped in disappointment as he tamped down the fury that flared and threatened to overrule his common sense.

"Rape is about power, dominance and fear. I've seen enough of them all in my lifetime that I don't need to take those from a woman." He scowled and walked toward her. "Sex has never been in short supply; I don't have to steal pussy."

She ducked her head.

He hadn't meant to sound gruff. But rape? Best tell her something to bring her mind to real time. "I ran the streets of Detroit with some friends. Not my partners, but some dudes from my neighborhood." He sat next to her.

"We did some small stuff, picked a couple of purses, stole from a few local stores. Nothing major. I got caught, went to juvie, dropped out of school and hung out with some friends. I played around with drugs, did some running and got into fights. The last time they picked me up, I was about sixteen. My mom refused to get me out. She'd told me the next time I got in trouble she'd leave me in there to learn responsibility." Those events happened so long ago; it felt like he spoke of someone else doing those things. He'd been a kid playing grown up, in a hurry to be legal. What a bunch of crap!

"Usually there's something that starts someone on a path like that," she said tentatively, a frown marring her brow.

He shrugged, noticing he had her full attention. Figures, he came as close as he ever had to baring his heart with a woman and she just stares. Tell her his early life's story and she's responsive.

"My mom worked all the time, my dad too. My brother and sister are eight and seven years older than I am. They had their own thing going on, and didn't watch me when they were supposed to. So I played outside late, spent time at friends and one day I met a man that everyone said I favored."

"Whaaat?"

He leaned back on the couch, and settled in for the telling. Journeys into his past weren't his most popular pastime. It'd been years since he'd thought about his mom's actions, and how the knowledge shaped his life.

"My mom had an affair and I was the result." Strange how after all these years he could say it plainly without the shame that had accompanied it for years.

"Oh, Ross," she whispered, moving closer to him on the sofa. He stiffened, refusing her pity. The small strokes her hand made on his arm, those he appreciated.

"The older I got, the more distant my dad, or my mom's husband became." He looked at the wall. "I didn't understand why he stopped playing games with me, or ruffling my hair, or talking to me. It was like a switch turned off and I ceased to exist for him." Pain he'd thought long gone resurfaced and ricocheted through his chest. He closed his eyes.

"It's okay, baby. I'm sorry I mentioned it." She hugged him around his shoulders. He relaxed into her warmth as the lingering pain drained away.

"No, actually I never thought his rejection started me acting out. I'd always been good in school. One day it just didn't matter. I quit." They sat quietly for a moment.

"Sometimes I analyze things to death." Cherise squeezed his shoulder and released him. "No child is responsible for the actions of his parents. You had nothing to do with what your mom did. The abuse they heaped on you, by ignoring you, is criminal."

He smiled at the heat in her voice. His heart had broken from what he considered a betrayal of the highest order. He'd been cold and untouchable since then.

Until now.

"At any rate, while I was detained, my counselor talked about the training programs. Inmates are required to choose a field. I liked working with my hands and anything requiring a suit or office was out. I entered the building program, learned construction and when I got released I apprenticed with an electrician and then a plumber." He threw his arm around her shoulders and pulled her close.

"Wasn't that hard?" She snuggled closer. He inhaled her natural scent and relaxed.

"Extremely. I had no life. But I had a plan. I wanted to own my company, make a lot of money, and leave the streets behind. For the most part, I've reached my goals." He took her smaller hand in his and kissed the back. "You still going to Lansing?"

"Yeah. A little later, though."

He smiled. "We cool?"

Cherise glanced around her small apartment. Her overnight bag still sat near the door, she could hear muted noise from her neighbor's television, everything seemed the same but was different.

A part of her felt like a fraud. Earlier, she'd left in a huff because he hadn't shared something she felt was critical info. Ross was right. Who determined when the time was right to open your closet of skeletons?

She couldn't. Not yet.

Her anxiety disorder loomed as Mt. Everest in her mind. She'd made progress, but the thought of his rejection because of her problem, sent a sharp radiating pain through her body. Each time she'd formed her lips to explain her condition, nausea and vertigo viciously assaulted her. The last time she tried to explain, the attack had been so bad, Ross carried her to bed, ordered her to her lay down and gave her a pain pill. She'd punked out and kept her silence.

"Yeah, we're cool." She nodded. "You'll be leaving soon and this is getting deep, at least for me. I need to focus on finishing my thesis and doing the job interviews."

He lifted her chin and stared into her eyes. "You wanna break this off? Is that what you're saying?" She pulled away.

"That's not what I said." She frowned. "I need to refocus on my goals and stuff. The last few weeks I've been off with my work, my class work I mean." It was too hard to think with him sitting so close, smelling good and feeling so warm.

He took a deep breath. "Damn" Pulling his hands behind his head, he closed his eyes.

Slanting sideways, her eyes roved over his body. His shirt stretched over his tight abs and chest. Pointed nipples stood at attention under his shirt, begging her to nibble and play. She'd missed him.

"Finished?"

She jumped at his voice. "What?"

"Never mind." He straightened and gazed at the blank television. "Why do we have to stop seeing each other? Lapeer's not that far, you'll be out of school soon, you can move closer."

She snorted.

"Or I'll move closer. Either way, we can still be together." He touched her face and she turned into his palm. "I don't want this to be over. Let's try and make it work." His fingers stroked her face.

Her heart leapt. She nodded, hiding her smile while taking his hand. "Missed me?" she whispered into his palm, and then bit down lightly on the flesh.

"Every minute." He took in short sips of air as her hand moved over his chest and gently flicked his nipple.

"Want me?" Her teeth scraped the tight buds through his shirt. She smiled as he shuddered beneath her palms.

"All the time."

"Take me."

Ross lifted and flipped her beneath him before the words were completely out of her mouth. He latched onto her lips and then wrestled her tongue into submission.

Her hands itched to touch him and roved over his back, pulling his shirt up. She craved the touch of his flesh. Skin to skin, she shoved her hand down the back of his jeans and cupped his ass. The belt held fast and needed to go.

Pushing up, she tried unbuckling, Ross slapped her hands away and undressed, but not before she slid her pants and top off. The heat from his eyes emboldened her, she cupped her full breast, held one to his mouth, while tugging the nipple of the other. He latched on with a wild hunger as her leg gave out under the pleasure.

He caught and laid her on the floor without releasing the nipple. His other hand investigated the wet warmth between her legs, teasing first her clit and then sliding two fingers into her sopping wet cunt.

"Ohhhh," she moaned while riding his fingers and holding his head to her breast. The pleasure spiked her core. Rational thought packed its bag and left town, emotional and physical gratification ruled. The nipple popped from his mouth, he moved south.

Her breaths shortened, her limbs tightened, her clit tingled in preparation for the crème de la crème. The man ate pussy like a gourmet meal and her body lay primed in preparation. He started slow, as if the clit and her outer lips were his favorite appetizer. Her toes curled as her hands tightened in his hair.

His fingers continued tunneling, in, out, driving her closer to the edge. He blew lightly on her sensitive clit, coaxing, teasing and then sucking as she bucked. The wave built from her toes, traveled up her back and she exploded in his mouth. Her legs trembled. Vaguely she heard his lapping and humming sounds. Her breath caught as the pleasure flared, her man sure did love to eat.

Chapter 10

Weeks later, Cherise sat stunned at the kitchen table watching Ross cook breakfast. He'd had a board meeting of some sorts at the last minute yesterday, and they'd arrived at his house in Lapeer late last night. She'd been too tired to see much of anything then. After getting a good look at his large home in the gated community, she was speechless.

During to the impromptu tour he'd taken her on, she learned there were four bedrooms. Five full baths and two half baths. The first floor boasted of all the formal living areas, including a library, office, atrium and enclosed heated pool. He kept surprising and leaving her speechless.

"I still don't understand why you bought such a large house. It's just you and from what you tell me, you spend very little time here," she said looking out the glass door to the lanai and pool area.

"It's an investment. With the economy the way it is, I was able to get a good deal on it. I added the wet areas–pool, sauna and whirlpool. Upgraded the kitchen and baths with some things we had at the office. Didn't cost much, but when the economy changes again I'll sell it at a profit. Until then, I live here and maintain it." He shrugged, and placed the sausage in the pan.

The aroma of sausage and eggs filled the room. From the corner of her eye, she watched as he moved around the space, pulling out plates and placing fruit in a bowl on the stone countertops. She'd offered to help, but he declined, insisting she sit so he could serve her.

"My grandma would kill for a kitchen like this."

"Your grandma? What about you?"

She looked around the bright space, noting the gleaming appliances and dark wood cabinets. He had good taste, much better than hers. But kitchens had never really been her thing.

"I don't spend enough time in this room to appreciate all the stuff you have in here." She waved at the juicer and dehydrator on the countertop. "Do you know what to do with these?"

"I use the juicer whenever I'm home and the dehydrator is Ms. Connie's. She left it here; I need to get it back to her. I use all the appliances I buy. Cooking relaxes me, so I enjoy it when I have time." He smiled. "Don't worry baby, we won't starve, I'll take good care of you." His tongue slowly licked his lips. He winked.

It took her a moment to remember Ms. Connie was his office manager, the wife of one of his mentors. Ross had been fortunate so many people took an interest in him along the way.

"Do all of you live in investment homes?" she asked, wanting to learn more about him.

"Hmmm, everyone lives in a gated community. Smoke has a large waterfront condominium and Red has a three-bedroom townhouse. They've lived in them longer than I've been here. This is my fourth house in ten years."

"What? That's a lot of moving around. You got some gypsy in you?"

Gypsy?" He asked startled.

She laughed.

"Nah, not that I know of anyway. I buy homes with resale potential. I know you realize the market in Michigan has been off for a while."

She nodded and drank a little of her juice.

"Well, I noticed that early on. The first house I bought had been in a fire, but the neighborhood was an up and coming one. I paid ten thousand for the property, put in another ten, including major demolition and added another five hundred square feet for a master suite. I lived there for two and a half years."

"How much did you sell it for?" she asked, totally blindsided by his business skills. This facet of his personality fascinated her. He obviously took his trade seriously. His eyes had taken on a gleam of excitement, his head all but thrown back, shoulders straight as he explained.

"I sold it for one hundred and ninety eight thousand, net."

"Net?" She blinked, not fully understanding his words.

"What I walked away with. The sales price was more, but after all the additional the fees are taken out, you have your net profit. That's what you take to the bank. I'd already bought another house and was working on it in my spare time." He brought their plates to the table.

"Back then I worked seven days a week, ten to twelve hours a day."

After offering a silent blessing over her food, she dug in. The eggs were perfect, with just the right amount of cheese and butter. She moaned in appreciation and licked a speck of food from her lips. If he kept cooking like this, she'd never leave.

Ross shook his head and started eating. "You should only make that face when we're making love, girl. You'll make me jealous."

"Ha, ha," she muttered and moaned louder after her next bite. Pointing her fork at him, she asked, "Why'd you work every day?"

"Rubie, my mentor from the prison, helped me get on a fast track to get my master electrician's and plumber's license. It was part of our big plan. "

She nodded, intrigued.

"I trained, got both my master electrician's and master plumber's licenses. It took ten years, working all the time to get the hours in both fields, but I did it. Red and Smoke journeyed under me. This way we could get paid for real."

She stared at him. "Get paid? What difference does it make?" She leaned back at the disbelieving look he sent. "What? I don't understand, you don't have to look at me like that, just explain."

He nodded. "Check this out. When a house or building is made, it has different parts." He looked at her, a devious smile lit his face. "Kinda like a woman's body."

She nodded, loving this playful side of him.

"A man should bring a few different skills to his…lady. It takes a variety to make the, um, relationship strong. You feel me?" His eyes were bright as he struggled to hold his laugh.

With a twist of her lips, she nodded, appreciating his

humor.

"Well, a general contractor pulls different trades together to make sure the building is put together the right way. You have your carpenters, plumbers, electricians, heating and air, brick masons, roofers, insulation and so forth. Follow me?"

"Yeah." Although she didn't know all the jobs he mentioned, she could tell he enjoyed sharing and she liked listening to him.

He nodded. "A talented man manages things, makes life as easy for his woman as possible, keeps everything running smooth. He provides whatever is needed." He winked.

"Seriously, the general contractor is like a manager, scheduling all the jobs, making sure everyone gets paid, overseeing the plans and shit. Well, what happens if you're the general contractor with your own carpenters, plumbers, electricians, heating and air, and brick masons? How much money could you save or make?"

He stared at her, waiting.

She shrugged. "A lot?" She guessed. "I don't know."

"Take the custom house in Big Lakes that you saw."

She nodded.

"All the electrical work for that house, including the elevator, is around two hundred thousand. The entire plumbing, about three hundred fifty thousand because of all the waterfalls and extra stuff. The heating and air, special order block work for the walls, custom roof, custom carpentry, wine cellar and shit adds up to a couple million dollars."

Her eyes rounded. She choked on the juice she'd just drank. Coughing she fanned her face while struggling to get her bearings.

"Well, we keep all that except the landscaping which we sub out. Take out the materials and we keep the rest. That's why we get paid."

"Oh…okay. Do you ever hire outside your group?"

"Not so much now. We have talented men who work for us. Almost a hundred percent ex-cons. We pay salaries, decent money with health insurance, bonuses, retirement and paid vacations. No matter what, my people are assured a stable income, which is why we have little turnover and serious loyalty."

"Do they all come from the program you were in?" She munched on the fruit salad as she waited for his answer.

"Yep, Rubie, that's the guy that started me in training, is still in charge. He sends me his best, or at least he used to."

"What?"

"Nothing, never mind. Just some things going down at work."

He placed the dishes in the sink, and ran water over them. She watched this domestic side of him, wondering who taught him.

Her man had a lot going for him, nice house, big ass Mercedes in the garage, successful company and community involvement. But if marriage wasn't in his future, where could their relationship go?

"Once I realized I could make a lot of money legally, I wanted to do it. Prison is a jacked up place but it taught me a few good things. Selling drugs or getting involved in shit where you have to watch your back all the time, hiding in the daylight; coming out like roaches at night is no way to live."

"Really, Ross, roaches? I'm eating here." She pushed the bowl of fruit away.

"Sorry about that, babe." He chuckled at her frown and grabbed her hand.

"Finish telling me what happened." She pouted and crossed her arms enjoying their early quiet time.

"The first time I took a job to build a custom house, may have been for someone in an organization. Lots of brick and block work, special order thick windows and glass. It was nice. I never saw the owner, although I heard he came by every day to look at the job. We finished ahead of time, with praises from the building inspectors and architect. That job was the turning point for us. The architect gave us lots of work, which in turn caused other architects to want to use us. Now, even in this economy, we're booked until next year with a waiting list if anything cancels."

He moved forward, pulled her from the table, and wrapped his arms around her. "My business is legal. We don't rip anybody off. Eventually, we'll buy a few acre tracts and build homes, three of which will be ours. We don't plan to do this forever. It's our ticket out for now. Investments and other things will sustain us in the future." He kissed her forehead.

Pulling back, he looked down into her eyes. "Trust me, baby, I won't do anything to hurt you. I know you're concerned. Yes, I have some money, but I earned every penny working with my hands. And I'm proud of it." Leaning forward, he captured her lips and deepened the kiss. She pushed into him, savoring his warmth and strength.

"I'm proud of you too," she murmured into his mouth.

Recognition slammed into her. This mattered. Who he was now, the wonderful, loving man he'd become. Stroking his back, she appreciated his strength of focus and commitment to his friends. Most importantly, she loved his determination to make this relationship work. She vowed to step up and work just as hard.

###

Cherise twirled, enjoying the band and Ross's sexy moves on the dance floor. The man didn't dance as much as bumped and grind up on her to the beat of the music. She loved every minute of it.

"Having fun?" he whispered into her ear, pulling her with him towards the drink area.

"Actually, I am. Everything's so pretty and the food is good. Not to mention, all the women are checking out my man and giving me the evil eye." She laughed at the red that crept up his neck. She couldn't take it back since it was true, and he knew it was. He'd been using her as a shield most of the evening, holding her hand tight, kissing her openly. She saw the disappointment and outright jealousy on the faces of some of the women.

"Naw, they were jealous of that dress you got on baby and the body beneath that's making it sing. I said earlier you were a fire hazard. You're smoking hot tonight," he countered, kissing her cheek.

He'd been grabbing and rubbing up on her all night. Her mom said every woman should have at least one classy kick ass dress in her closet and she did. Tonight she wore a honey colored sheath that dipped low in the back, showing skin and clung to every part of her. Her hair was up in a messy do, with curls framing her face. Her three-inch heels included the same color of her dress along with other earth tones. Ross's hand rested possessively on her bare back, stroking it with light touches, sending a slight tremor through her. The wicked look in his eye said he knew the effect he had on her and enjoyed it.

"Where's Red and Smoke?" she asked, moving away to get her bearings. He was hell on her system; her body was constantly on alert for more foreplay.

Ross looked around the room and nodded. "They're over there near the drinks with Julio and Rubie." He paused. "Have you met him?"

"No, not yet." He pulled her toward a middle-aged man with a full head of salt and pepper hair. The man looked small standing next to Red and Smoke. His posture, hands stuffed in his pockets, reminded her of Michael Douglas. His eyes were animated as he laughed at a comment Smoke made.

The three of them stopped talking as she drew near. She wondered what had Red's jaw so tight. Ross squeezed her hand before releasing it to give his partners a fist pound. He shook hands with the older man and turned to her.

"Cherise, I want you to meet another member of our

administration, Benjamin Rubinowitz, better known as Rubie." He nodded in the man's direction. "Rubie, my lady, Cherise."

"It's so nice to meet you, my dear," Rubie said taking her hand and holding it in both of his. "Ross and these young men are like sons to me. I'm so proud of them and glad my boy had the sense to claim a woman as beautiful as you." He squeezed her hand, leaned forward and kissed her cheek.

"Thank you," she breathed, trying not to tense up. Invasion of her personal space was still an area of challenge for her, although not as debilitating as it once was. "Ross has told me a lot of good things about you. I'm glad you were there to help him get started."

Rubie nodded and smiled. "Trust me, the pleasure was and is mine." He turned and looked at Red and Smoke.

"We can get together tomorrow and talk. Tonight, let's enjoy this expensive party." The men nodded. Rubie smiled and walked off.

"No wonder he ran, here comes Ms. Connie," Ross said under his breath. She couldn't tell if he was pleased or pissed. Red and Smoke disappeared as well.

"Who?" She asked, turning in the direction he looked. A small woman of indiscriminate age walked up to them. Her eyes were lit from within, as if she laughed at a joke she alone knew. Her smile was kind as she extended her hand.

"Ross, you look real handsome in that suit. I always said you boys cleaned up nice." The older woman leaned up, offering her cheek and hands to him.

He kissed her cheeks, reddening further. "Thanks, Ms. Connie. " He turned towards Cherise. "I want you to meet my lady, Cherise. Cherise, this is Ms. Connie. I told you about her, she runs our office and tries to run our lives. She still calls us boys." He held onto Ms. Connie's hands while she tried to hit him.

They laughed.

"Nice to meet you, Ms. Connie." Up close, the woman favored Louise Jefferson. Short, stuffed up top and a large warm smile. Cherise's eyes widened, as she was unceremoniously pulled forward into a hug and a kiss on the cheek.

"We don't stand on ceremony round here. I call all these boys mine. So if you're with him, I want to know you better. Welcome to the family."

"Uh…thank you, ma'am." Cherise watched Ross turn away, with a smile on his face. Enduring the embrace, she hid her grimace. She'd never been a touchy, feely person with strangers, and wholeheartedly believed in personal space.

"Come over here, Cherise, let's talk for a minute and get to know each other better." The woman may have been small, but the grip on her arm let her know it wasn't a suggestion. Looking at Ross, she winced as he shrugged his shoulders and looked away.

Chicken.

"Yes ma'am." What else could she say or do? She didn't want to run the risk of hurting or offending the older woman by snatching out of her grasp. Like a meek mouse, she allowed herself to be pulled to a nearby table.

Erosa Knowles- Men of 3X CONStruction
Book 1

"Wait a minute, I think that's Denise." The older woman squinted and looked around a few bodies until she was satisfied. "Yep, that's her. I'll be damned. There'll be some fireworks here tonight," she muttered.

Cherise looked into the crowded room, searching for the person that had set off the woman. But since she didn't know who Denise was, she sat and waited. Her eyes landed on the man standing next to Smoke. He was gorgeous with a little Asian, Latin and possibly something else mixed in his heritage. Tall and tan, nice body, she wondered if he'd been in prison as well. She made a mental note to ask Ross later.

"Denise...Denise!" Ms. Connie shouted and waved, gaining the attention of a rich mocha-skinned woman. Smiling a greeting, the woman headed in their direction. Cherise watched as the two women embraced, and walked towards the table. Pasting a smile on her face, she waited for an introduction.

"Denise, it's so good to see you. I'm glad you came." Ms. Connie hugged the woman again and turned to her.

"Denise, meet Cherise. Cherise, meet Denise."

Cherise stood and shook the offered hand. "Hi, how are you," she murmured taking in the dimpled smile and clear, dark brown eyes.

"I'm good, thanks. How are you?"

"Okay, thanks." Pleasantries aside, Cherise waited for more information on the identity of the woman. She tuned into the conversation.

"Denise, how are the twins?" Ms. Connie asked, touching the other woman's hand.

"Terrorists in disguise." A tinkling laugh flowed

from her lips. "I love them, though. They started preschool and are trying to run the class. I get a phone call from their teacher every week about something or other." She waved away Ms. Connie's concern and questions.

"Trust me, they love having the girls and wouldn't want them any other way. I tried to pull them once and had a major fight on my hands, from both the girls and their teacher." She smiled.

Cherise was stunned at the news. No way could this young woman be a mother to twins. She looked to young.

"Terrorists, hmpf… I saw them last month and they were beautiful, well behaved—" Ms. Connie stopped at the raised brow from Denise.

They laughed.

Cherise cringed when Ms. Connie patted Denise's hand again. Was all the touching necessary? She kept the smile pasted on her face and listened politely, hoping to learn more.

"Yeah, you got them pegged right, Denise. I was only with them for about thirty minutes. Exhausted is the best word describing how I felt when they left to go home." She patted Denise's hand again and turned to face Cherise.

"You've met Red? "

Cherise nodded, confused at the question.

"Those are his twins; hopefully you'll get to meet them. Shannon and Shantel, they're four and a handful. They keep all of us on our toes." Smiling, the older woman patted Denise's hand for the umpteenth time.

Cherise's eyes widened at the news of Red being a

father. Never in a million years would she have pegged him in that role.

"Denise, Cherise is dating Ross." She paused. "He introduced her as his woman."

Denise's mouth dropped open. And just as Cherise's temper rose, Denise broke into a laugh, jumped up and ran to hug her.

"It's about damn time!"

These people had no regard for personal space.

Unsure of the comment or the arms surrounding her, Cherise offered a small smile. Watching both women, she waited for them to explain the remark.

"I know, it's great! Right?" Ms. Connie agreed, clapping her hands.

Denise returned to her seat. "I told him it would hit him hard one day. He laughed. Girl, I hope you gave him a good run. The man is too cocky by half."

Cherise smiled, liking the woman. "He is that, but I don't know if this is what you think it is."

Ms. Connie grunted and took a sip of water from her glass. Leaning forward, she waved the two women forward. "Sweetie, he has never introduced a woman to me as his woman, girlfriend, squeeze or lay of the moment." She chuckled at her joke.

Cherise's brow furrowed as she thought about the comment. Did they think that was good news? Ross was thirty; didn't they think it strange he played the field that long? She did.

Denise nodded in agreement. "I've only known them about five and a half years. Lots of women have hit on him and Lord knows the man is color blind. He's probably dated every color and ethnicity there is, but he has never had a serious relationship, said he didn't believe in them."

"But it was his idea," Cherise said, without realizing what she'd let slip. Both women stared at her in awe, or admiration, she couldn't be sure. "I mean, we talked about it and he said he wanted to be exclusive—" She stopped when their eyes widened.

"What?" she asked.

"Ross, in a monogamous relationship. Sweetie, that's great news. I'm so happy." Ms. Connie's eyes misted over while she reached forward, and grabbed her hand, squeezing it slightly.

Denise sent her a shy smile, excused herself from the table, and merged with a group of people talking nearby. A few moments later, she stormed to the table, Red fast on her heels.

Ross materialized and pulled out the chair next to Cherise. She jumped in surprise.

"You okay?" he whispered, pulling her close and throwing an arm around her shoulders.

"Yeah," she whispered. "Red has kids and a woman?"

"Old drama. Kind of a love-hate relationship. I don't think either of them can move on." He shrugged. "You ready to go?" he asked.

His eyes held the promise of a night filled with hot, leisurely loving. She squeezed her thighs together. Every part of her responded to his suggestion. She licked her lips.

"Whenever you are." She rubbed his face and leaned forward for a kiss. He took her lips, bit the bottom one lightly and deepened the kiss. She forgot where they were, who was around. Nothing mattered but the taste of this man. They broke apart, panting. She pulled him close and was about to claim another kiss when a cough caught her attention.

Smoke stood at the table watching them with a sad smile.

"Ross, I hate to bother you with this, but the Mayor wants to talk with the three of us about some type of project. Rubie's talking to him right now. If you can't, I'll blow him off with some excuse." He turned, looked back. "On second thought, they're headed this way. Let's make this quick."

"Back in a minute, then we're outta here." Ross gave her a quick peck on her lips and rose. She wasn't accustomed to public displays of affection, but Ross had no problems letting her know how he felt, at any time, any place. It was as though no one else mattered besides them. She loved it.

Red stole a kiss from Denise, squeezed her hand and left, leaving her staring at his back. Cherise knew no matter what the woman said, she was in love with Red.

"Well, Cherise, I think you've accomplished what so many others have tried and failed at. Ross is in love." Denise smiled at her proclamation.

"I don't know about that," she said.

A wave of pleasure washed over her at Denise's words. It felt good knowing his friends thought this was special for Ross. He'd come to mean so much to her, she'd hate to be out there by herself.

"Red will never give you up, Denise. Why don't you try and work things out?" Ms. Connie asked gently.

"Why do you assume I'm the problem? Red may not want to let me move on, but he won't commit to me, either. I'm tired of waiting for him to grow up. I want a normal life. A regular date with someone that appreciates me, loves me and only me!" She stood as tears filled her eyes.

"If I have to put a restraining order on his ass I will! Because I'm ready to move on and have an adult relationship, more kids, a real family. And despite what you may think, Ms. Connie, Red doesn't want that."

"How do you know what I want? You won't even talk to me." Red's deep voice spoke from behind Denise. She spun around and faced him. Her hand flew to her mouth as she stepped back. He grabbed her hand, pulled her behind him and walked away.

Ms. Connie sighed as Ross walked over to the table, took Cherise's hand and assisted her to stand. Bending down, he kissed Ms. Connie's cheek, while Cherise waited to embrace the woman. All in all, tonight had been informative.

"Ready for me?" Ross murmured in her ear as they waited for the valet to bring car.

"Always," she whispered, snuggling into his embrace.

Chapter 11

Ross left the reception area in the main office after giving Cathy, Rubie's niece, an inventory list. Somehow, the company paid for items they didn't need and worse, couldn't find after delivery. Red's initials were on a few of the orders. He made a mental note to talk to his partner about those supplies.

"How was the gala last month?" Cathy smiled coyly, following him. Thank God, she had a crush on Red. The high nasal pitch of her voice was annoying.

"Fine, everyone seemed to have a nice time." In general, he avoided the thin bottle-bleached blonde whenever possible, choosing to wait and deal with Ms. Connie. Cathy looked emaciated and spindly to him. Her smiles never reached her eyes; and she set off his bullshit meter big time.

His cell vibrated. Thinking it was Cherise, he answered without looking at the ID and shut his office door.

"Hey baby."

"Ross, I need you to take Lenora for a while."

"Who's this? Lenora who?" Confused over the request, he moved toward his desk and sat.

"Damn, I really fucked up by keeping her away from you. This is Pam and Lenora is your l'il girl, our l'il girl."

He froze as recollections flipped through his mind. Five, or was it four years ago, Social Services contacted him about being a deadbeat dad. Hell, he'd only seen Pam once before that call, and he was drunk at a party at the time. He started to ask how she got his number but realized it didn't matter. She wanted him to watch Lenora, something must be wrong.

"Why? Is there a problem?" He asked, instead. She'd never allowed him to see the child since they went to court to prove he was the father. Butterflies swarmed his stomach as the reality hit him.

"Yeah, but I don't want to get into it right now. Hopefully, I can get it straightened out soon. I just need you to take her for a day or two. I'll call you, and let you know when to bring her home."

"Let me get this straight, and pardon me for not trusting this whole set-up." His tone dry. "You want me to pick up Lenora, my daughter, who you've never let me see before? And she's supposed to stay with me for a few days? That sounds like bullshit."

"Yeah Ross. I'm sorry about being such a bitch before. I guess I was mad at the time. But you've always done right by her. The checks always came from the courts on time."

"Um, okay. I'm supposed to get involved now why?" He wasn't buying this five year down the road change of heart.

"I don't have anyone else I can trust with her."

"You don't know if you can trust me. Shit we only met that one time. You need to talk true and cut to the chase. I don't have time for games."

She sighed long into the silence. "I might be in some trouble and I need to clear it up. But I need to make sure my baby's taken care of first. Please Ross; I need you to take her for a day or two."

Hell, what could he do? "All right, give me your address and I'll pick her up on my way out tomorrow."

"Where are you headed?"

"My girlfriend's graduating from college tomorrow. I'm on my way there."

Silence.

"I know I have no right to say anything. But don't let nothing happen to my baby, okay?"

Ross looked at the phone. "Don't start tripping. Ain't nobody going to hurt her! Give me the address and have her packed. I'll swing by early in the morning."

Although he wanted to meet his daughter, he wouldn't bow to Pam. She'd stolen years of his daughter's life from him already. He wondered if he'd be seeing his child now if she didn't need a favor. Probably not.

"Sometimes women get jealous and take it out on the child, don't front like you ain't never heard of that kind of thing happening before. "

"My woman's got me. No reason for her to be jealous. Now, do you want me to pick her up or not? I got a lot to do before heading out." He didn't like her accusations. She didn't know him or Cherise.

"Yeah, here's my address."

###

Ross looked up at the one and a half story house. Nice neighborhood, he thought. Climbing out of his truck, he took in the well-manicured lawns, and fenced yards with swings and bikes. The calm scene didn't dispel the sense of unease he'd felt since Pam called him yesterday.

He'd never expected to hear from her again since she'd
told him he would never see his daughter. Most of all,
he'd been shocked she had his number all this time.
Enough procrastinating, he needed to get on the road, his
baby graduated in a few hours.

After taking a few steps toward the yard, the feeling
of dread increased. He stopped and looked over the house
again. It was quiet, too quiet. His eyes rested on the
porch, a plant was over-turned, and dirt scattered across
an otherwise immaculate area.

He frowned and walked forward. From this angle he
noticed the front door stood open and hung off the hinges.
Soft sounds emanated from within. Caution won over
heroics.

Shit!

"Pam," he called out from the edge of the porch, not
wanting to draw too much attention. Damn, he knew too
many guys that'd made the mistake of marching into a
situation that looked shitty and got nailed. He pulled his
cell out and called 911.

###

"He's not gonna make it," Cherise said soberly,
looking around the crowded auditorium. She'd planned to
spend her graduation day with her two favorite people,
her mom and Ross.

"Your nose is so wide open a truck could drive
through!" her mom chortled.

"No, Mom, he's a good man and I really like him,"
she'd countered, biting her lower lip. But she suspected
her mom knew the truth. She was so over the top with this

man, it scared her. Sleep eluded her, unless she was partially covered by his large frame. Their daily noon check-ins were manna for her. She *needed* to hear from him, talking, laughing and although she'd never admit it, she craved being in his presence. *Not good.*

While stretching her neck to see over the heads of the people filling the auditorium, she pulled her lip between her teeth. Trepidation filled her heart.

"Something's wrong." She could taste it.

"You don't know that, baby girl, he may just be running a l'il late," her mom answered while fussing with her robe and handing her the tassel for her cap.

"Not for this, mama. Not for my graduation." She shook her head. "Besides, Ross is never late, for anything. I'm not over-analyzing or working myself into frenzy. I'm stating a fact."

She paused looking around, knowing he would've found her by now if he'd been in the building. Only something major would cause him to miss her big day.

Where was he? *Please God, let him be all right.*

"I'm going to go in, line up," she said, her voice dripping with disappointment.

She'd agreed to move in with him until she decided which direction to go. Most of her stuff had been packed. Two days ago, he'd left to bring a company truck to move her. Last night he'd called saying he had a stop to make and then he'd head out to her graduation.

The hand on her shoulder stopped her. "Listen to me, Cherise Renée Walters."

She froze, whenever her mom used all three of her names, it was not for kicks and giggles.

"Yes, ma'am?"

Her mom's eyes softened. "Baby, this *is your* day. Your dreams are unfolding before your eyes. Never give someone so much power they can destroy something that means so much to you. He's not graduating in the top ten percent of his class today. You are. Be proud of that! If no one was here to share it with you, know for sure you reached a personal milestone for yourself. This is your day, and you're the only one who can allow someone else to ruin it. Don't give anyone that much control, baby.

Cherise nodded.

After lining up, she realized there'd been no signs of a panic attack. She stiffened her spine. She had so much to be grateful for today.

###

"Ross, the police want to talk to you again. Hopefully, we can get out of here after this," his attorney called out to him from the other office. He hung up the phone at the police station in frustration. Cherise hadn't answered her cell and her voicemail was full. He needed to talk to her.

He missed her graduation. Damn! His fist clenched in anger.

He wanted to throttle that bitch Pam. She'd drawn him into some shit he no idea was going down. The only redeeming thing about it all was she protected her children. Lenora hadn't been in the house during the attack. She'd been at the neighbors waiting for him. Unfortunately, he had no idea, and left when the police arrived.

Erosa Knowles- Men of 3X CONStruction
Book 1

He hated not being able to talk to Cherise, tell her what was happening and let her know he'd be there to move her as soon as this bullshit settled.

"I'm coming," he snapped at his attorney, who'd returned to get him. Pam's situation may be important to the police, but talking to Cherise was critical for him. Red and Smoke were out checking into some things, his cell lay dead in his truck. And his woman wasn't answering her phone. He hoped everything went okay at the graduation. Switching off the light, he moved into the hall and left the building.

###

"Cherise, are you sure you don't want to go on the cruise with me? It's not until next weekend. We can paint the town before the real world intrudes," her mom offered later that night. They'd gone to dinner to celebrate and returned to her apartment. Looking around, she decided to finish packing tomorrow. Her heart was too sick to do anything right now. She patted her pocket, making sure her phone was there and on vibrate. Moving a few boxes, she sat them on the floor and flopped on the sofa.

"You want something to drink?"

"No thanks, Mom, I'm good." She picked up the remote and turned on the TV.

"I'm gonna warm up my leftovers from the restaurant, you want yours?"

"No, maybe later, I'm not—damn!"

She heard her mom's footsteps moving towards the living room. "What? What's wrong?"

Cherise pointed to the television, her mouth open, eyes wide in shock. "That's Ross, he was arrested earlier today."

"Whaaat? Are you sure?" Her mom dropped besides her taking the remote and flipping channels until another news station reported the incident.

In a surprising turn of events, Ross Stemple of Three X Construction showed up at the Detroit police station this morning with his attorney in connection of the near-fatal beating of Pam Brown. It is believed Ms. Brown called out Mr. Stemple's name before losing consciousness. More on this as the story unfolds.

Cherise's lips trembled as she looked at her mom's shocked face. Blindly, she reached out and held her mom close. Tears ran unchecked down her cheek. A myriad of questions flew through her mind; she was too numb to voice them.

Ross in jail for beating a woman? *He wouldn't do that.* Who was this woman? Is she who he went to see before returning yesterday? Was he okay? Ms.Connie…she'd call Ms. Connie.

"I need to call Ms. Connie, Mama. She's the office manager. I need her to tell me what's going on."

Her mom nodded and returned to the kitchen. A few moments later, she heard her mom's voice and knew she was on the phone.

The line to Ross's office rang and rang, until it finally went to voice mail. "Ms. Connie, this is Cherise. I just saw the news about Ross, please call me on my cell and let me know what's going on." She left her number and hung up. Picking up the remote, she clicked through all the news channels, searching for more information,

Erosa Knowles- Men of 3X CONStruction
Book 1

anything.

Jumping up, she ran to her room and pulled out a suitcase. She started grabbing things she might need in the next few days on the bed.

"Ma...Mama" she called out. She'd need to borrow her mom's rental or go and pick up another one. She'd probably need to book a hotel room as well. Why hadn't her mom answered her? Holding her toiletry bag in one hand, she left her room in search of her mom. She found her leaning against the kitchen counter with the phone next to her ear. After maneuvering around a few boxes, she waited until she was done. When her mom looked up, there was sadness in her eyes, or was it pity?

Cherise's head snapped back. Her heart raced in preparation for bad news. The bag dropped unnoticed to the floor.

"What?" she whispered, needing to know, but wanting to hide until the worst passed. Her mom placed a finger to her lips, as she listened to the conversation. Cherise vibrated with fear and a need to know if Ross was all right.

"Okay, hey thanks, Gee. I owe you one," her mom spoke solemnly as she clicked off. Inhaling, her mom stared at her and waved her out the kitchen into the living room.

Oh shit, it must be bad.

"The woman in question," her mom said after they sat on the sofa. "Is Pam Brown. She was beaten and is in critical condition. They aren't sure she'll make it. It seems she has three kids. One of them a little girl named Lenora. Lenora Stemple in fact."

"Stemple...Stemple, as in Ross Stemple?!"
Impossible!

Her mom nodded. "For some reason Ms. Brown was moaning and calling his name when the police and paramedics came. Once the connection was realized, they put out an APB on him. Strange enough he was in town and turned himself in. There's a lot of speculation, but not a whole lot of concrete information yet."

"Ma, are you telling me Ross, my Ross, has a daughter? She couldn't believe it. No way, no way would he have kept that from her.

Her mom nodded. "I'm afraid so, baby. I don't know the particulars, but that part is true. She's about four or five years old."

"Five years!" She shook her head. "I can't believe he didn't—"

Her mom placed her arms around her as she dropped her head into her palms. They sat like that for a few minutes.

"He didn't tell me about being an ex-con, ma."

"I know, baby."

"How could he not mention he had a kid?"

Her mom sighed and squeezed her tight. "I don't know him or his situation, so I can't answer that. You know him better, what do you think his reason might be?"

Cherise stood and turned towards her mom. "Oh, no! I'm not going to be rational about this, Mama. I cannot think of one reason to hide your child. Especially after the way he grew up, you'd think he'd know better. No, he doesn't get a pass on this!"

Erosa Knowles- Men of 3X CONStruction
Book 1

Her mom held her palms up and shrugged. "Okay, calm down, it's your life. I just asked a question. You of all people should know things aren't always the way they appear."

"Stop, Mama! We aren't talking about you or me! This is about Ross and his lying, omitting ass!"

"Cherise, I raised you better than this!" Her mom scowled. "You always need to look at both sides. Or at least admit there's a possibility of another side. Not go off half-cocked. That's how fools respond. And you're no fool." She paused. "Now think, why wouldn't he have told you about this child. A child that was a part of his life before he met you. Her mother lives in another city. The two of you have been dating for what two, three months?"

"Somewhere in between." It galled her, but her mom was right. Right now, she couldn't think of one reason good enough. There might be one, but it eluded her. *Damn it!*

"Has he ever gone to Detroit or mentioned a woman or child."

Cherise hated to think rationally. She wanted to throw a hissy fit. Unfortunately, her mama had never permitted them, even when she was a kid. "No, we spent our weekends together, either here or at his place in Lapeer. I can't remember him mentioning a child or another woman."

"Doesn't that strike you as strange?" Her mom watched her.

"It strikes me strange he never mentioned he had a child." Her mood soured, she was in no frame of mind to be generous.

"All right, isn't it odd he never went to visit or called the child or mother?"

"Just because he didn't call her around me, doesn't mean he didn't call. He was in Detroit and she knew he was coming or had been there. That's probably why she was calling out his name."

Her mom looked at her, and shook her head. "You've already convicted him. I'm glad you're not on the jury of any of my cases. Now, I don't know your Ross, never met him. But think. He was supposed to be here and he went there first. Maybe he was picking up the little girl and bringing her to the graduation. Maybe there was a problem and the mother called and asked him to come. Cherise, there are a lot of possibilities. Don't let your emotions carry you someplace your ass can't keep you."

"Why are you taking up for him? I'm your daughter! I'm the one hurting." Her head pounded. Nothing happened today as it should have. "This is supposed to be my big day!" she whispered. "I graduated and against the odds conquered my disorder. I want Ross, Mama."

Chapter 12

Cherise stretched as sunlight filtered into her bedroom. A dry burnt taste seared her tongue, she smacked her lips trying to remember what she'd eaten the night before. She rolled over, her hand searching for Ross before memories of last night slammed into her. Her heart dropped in tandem with her outstretched hand.

"Are you awake?" her mom's voice cut through the silence of the room.

"Hmmm, yes. What time is it? How long have I been asleep?"

"It's six o'clock in the morning; I'm going for my run. I wanted you to know before I left the house."

"Hold up, give me a minute and I'll go with you." Rolling out of bed she headed for the bathroom, after finishing there, she dressed quickly in sweats and met her mom in the living room, water bottle in hand.

"That was fast. I'm surprised." Her mom looked her over.

"Yeah I have a lot of things to get done today and wanted to start early. By the way, Daddy called last night and invited me down for a week this summer. He offered to match a thousand dollars with you to pay off my car as a graduation present."

Her mom nodded and smiled. "Sounds like a good idea."

"I need to apologize for last night. I know you always have my back. This thing with Ross has me tied up in knots. I don't want to be rational or understanding." They walked at a fast pace.

"Then drop him. If you don't want to hear his explanation, or you're not ready to deal with him, put your stuff in storage and leave. Deal with it when you're ready."

Cherise stopped, bent over and placed her hands on her knees. "Is that what you'd do?"

"No! I would want to know what the hell happened. Besides, I learned a long time ago how it feels to have someone bail out on you when the shit hits the fan. So no, I wouldn't do it. But Cherise," her mom touched her shoulder. "Look at me."

Straightening, she gazed into warm brown eyes, totally lacking in judgment.

"I'm an ex-stripper, who lived a wild life. You know the story, my family put me out at 16, when they found out I was pregnant. Even after I lost the baby, they had no forgiveness and refused to allow me to come home. I did what I had to, to survive. It was the luck of the draw when I met your daddy, new to the military and still country fresh. He wanted himself some Veronique and married me. He got me off the streets, but there's still some street in me. That's why I defend those who can't defend themselves. There's usually a reason people do the things they do. I don't make excuses; I merely wait until I have all the information before I decide. That's all I'm suggesting to you."

Pausing, she continued. "Are you ready to let him go for good? Cause playing games is a waste of time."

Cherise smiled, remembering a conversation from

last week. "I'm about as ready to let him go as you are to let my daddy go. You didn't tell me the two of you still connect on occasion. Uh-huh, he asked me if I wanted y'all to get back together."

"Really, what did you say?" Her mom's breath quickened.

"I told him I remembered what he did to my mama and I didn't want her to ever hurt like that again."

Her mom reached out and held her. Cherise sighed as gentle hands stroked her back. "Life's about living, baby. No one's perfect and everyone makes mistakes. Don't think loving someone means they'll never hurt you or mess up, because that's not true. We do our best to be fair, to do the right thing and not hurt anyone else. It doesn't always work out that way. But we are only charged to try, to do our best."

Cherise nodded. She and Ross had come a long way, but they still withheld a lot from each other. She wanted him to open up and expose his skeletons, but she was scared shitless to do the same. What if he was as worried of her reaction, as she was of his?

"Ma, let's get the boxes in storage, then I'm coming home with you for a little while. I'll take you up on the cruise. I'm not running. I'm just not ready to handle all this right now. By the time I get back, it'll almost be time for the wedding. And then I'll decide what I want to do."

Her mom nodded, "Okay, I'll race you back" she said and took off, Cherise running behind her.

###

"Cherise, your cell is ringing!" her mom yelled from the living room. They'd been in Colorado for a couple of days and were going shopping.

"Thanks, Ma!" she ran into the living room and picked it up.

"Hello."

"Hey, where are you?" Ross asked.

She collapsed onto the chair hearing his voice. Her heart leapt to her throat. It'd been too long. She ached for him. Once she decided she was leaving with her mom, she'd shut down. She hired some movers, shut down her apartment and turned off her cell. Last night, she powered it up, but was afraid to call him. She didn't think she could hear about another woman giving him a child, and him not telling her.

"I'm at my mom's in Colorado."

"Okay," he exhaled. "I'm sorry I missed your graduation. I went by your apartment earlier and noticed you'd already moved out. Are you moving to Colorado?"

"I'm not sure yet. I'll decide when I get back."

"Get back? Where are you going?"

"My mom's taking me on a cruise for my graduation. We're leaving at the end of the week."

"Ahhh, I see. Is this new? You hadn't mentioned a cruise before."

"Yeah, it's new."

"Hmmm, okay. You got a few minutes? I need to talk to you about something."

"Sure, what's up?" Her heart pummeled in her chest and her breaths shortened. She prayed for strength and a little bit of her mom's wisdom.

"I can tell you know some of what happened the day

Erosa Knowles- Men of 3X CONStruction
Book 1

you graduated, but not all of it. First off, I got a call from Pam telling me she was in trouble and wanted me to take Lenora for a while. I was surprised because I hadn't talked to her in over four years and she'd never let me see the child since court. So I said okay. I called and told you I had to make a stop. That was it. I had to pick up Lenora."

"Who's Lenora and Pam?"

"Lenora is my daughter. Pam's her mom."

"You never told me you had a child."

Silence filled the air.

"Why didn't you tell me?" She tried to keep the disappointment out of her voice, but failed.

"Truthfully? ... I didn't think about it one way or the other."

She coughed trying to respond to his outrageous comment.

"Hear me out, hear me out." He paused, and then continued when she didn't say anything. "I was out of town at some party, we met that night and had sex in the parking lot. Not pretty, but true. I swore I wore protection so when she contacted the guy who had the party and got my name, I balked. Demanded a paternity test. After she had the baby, Social Services got involved. The paternity test proved I was the father and she swore I'd never see the baby after we left court. My bank sends the court a check each month and forwards the money to her. I had no idea where she lived until she called the other day and told me."

"Why wouldn't she let you see your daughter?" Cherise was incensed when people played games with children.

"She was angry I didn't want anything to do with her. Hell, I didn't know her. I couldn't pick her out of a line-up. I've only seen Pam two times, including when she got pregnant and I was drunk at the time."

"Go ahead." This was getting worse. The man was clueless. Having a child definitely went into the need to know column along with ex-con status. *What about your mental treatments?* She squashed the thought.

He gave her a recap of the events that day.

"Didn't you call Red and Smoke?" she asked when he finished.

"Yeah, I did. They met me at my attorney's office.

Her heart sank. No one thought to call her. Common courtesy wasn't extended. They knew she expected him. Damn.

"You heard me?"

"No, what did you say?"

"I said my cell phone died. I called you from the attorney's office and the police station. Your voice mail was full so I couldn't leave a message."

"Hmmm."

"My attorney got the call they wanted me for questioning and we went in. It didn't take long to unravel. Since I never went into the house, there were no prints linking me to the crime. The real problems started the next day when Pam died."

"She died?"

"Yeah, I found out she had three kids, from different men. One of them has some sort of problem. Each of us paid child support, which allowed her to live in the nice neighborhood. From what I understand, she was a good mother and loved her kids."

"That's good to know." Cherise sensed bad news on the horizon. It shouldn't have taken three days to sort out this mess. Her stomach twisted in knots waiting for rest of the tale.

"Pam collected Social Security and child support. Her latest boyfriend is up on charges for the murder. They think he wanted some money and she refused. He wouldn't leave her alone, ignored the restraining order and that's when she called me."

"What happens now?"

"Lenora's a ward of the court, her grandparents are petitioning for custody. I'm discussing the best plan of action with my attorney."

"What do you mean the best plan of action? She's yours. She goes with you, what's there to discuss?" Surely, he didn't intend to give up his child. What kind of man did that?

"Hold up, check the attitude. What do I know about raising a child? I work all the time. I need to do what's best for her."

"Those are excuses, Ross. Whenever *you* want to do something, nothing and I mean nothing stands in your way. Don't tell me you can't do this. You can if you wanted to."

"I'm responsible— "

"She's your number one responsibility and I can't believe we are having this conversation."

"Damn it, Cherise— "

"You're not the man I thought you were if you can abandon your child again. She needs her family, she needs you."

"That not what I said. I need to talk—"

"We have nothing more to talk about."

She hung up and powered off her phone. Hurt mixed with anger flooded her. How could she have been so wrong about him? Five years! He missed being a part of his child's life, and he'd accepted that. Men could be so stupid.

Shaking her head, she had to leave this man alone, at least for now.

Ross looked at the phone and snapped it close. His lips and jaw tight, he walked over to the van and waved Red and Smoke towards the truck.

"She's already moved the boxes and furniture. Let's go home," Ross said. He snatched opened his door and sat behind the wheel. "Damn it!" he hit the wheel and jammed the key into the ignition, gunning the motor. Throwing the gear in reverse, he sped backwards and tore out of the parking lot.

He took a glance in his rear view mirror. Red and Smoke kept up. Good, in his mood he didn't want to babysit anybody. His phone rang. He picked it up knowing it wasn't the person he wanted to talk to.

"Yeah"

"Ross, I just checked the messages and thought you should know Cherise called the office wanting to know

what was going on. It was the day you were in Detroit."
Ms. Connie paused. "Ross! Did you hear me?"

"Yes, I heard you. It doesn't matter. She already blew
me off. I'm on my way back home. I have a lot to deal
with. Has my attorney sent over the package?"

"Yes," she answered hesitantly. "But I'm sure you
misunderstood. Cherise cares a lot for you."

He snorted.

"The two of you just have to talk, work it out."

"Yeah, sure." He rolled his eyes, deliberately pushing
his conversation with Cherise to the side. He'd deal with
it later or not at all. She kept running whenever there was
a problem, especially now, when he needed her most.
Maybe he was wrong and they'd moved too fast. At any
rate, he couldn't focus on that right now.

"Has Social Services called about my daughter? I
should've been there dealing with that instead of rushing
up here. Her grandparents want custody of her, but don't
have a pot to piss in themselves."

He remembered his first meeting with the older
woman and seedy man. Maybe it was because they had to
bury their child, but he read the greed on their faces. From
what he'd learned, Pam's brothers and sisters had taken
the furniture and clothes from her house before she'd
made it into the ground. They reminded him of parasites
and he didn't intend to allow his daughter to be in their
care.

"No, no one other than the attorney's office. You
know, Cherise's Masters' degree is in education." Ms
Connie continued, not ready to give it a rest. "She'd be a
big help getting Lenora settled."

"And so will a lot of other professionals. Right now, I have to focus on getting custody of Nora and fulfilling the building contracts we have. I'm on my way back in, have the team ready in the office first thing in the morning so we can go over our schedule and I can give assignments."

"Yes. sir!"

"Good, I'll see you in the morning." He hung up, ignoring her mocked salute.

Ross pressed a button on his phone.

"Mr. Jacobs' office."

"Hi, Helene, this is Ross Stemple. Is Brian in?"

"Yes, of course. One minute, please.

"Ross, this is a surprise. I didn't expect to hear from you for a day or two. Is everything all right?

"Yeah, everything's fine. Have you heard anything from the Social Worker?"

"She called earlier. It seems the grandparents want to fight for custody on this one. I don't understand it. They didn't even try to get any of the other children, in fact, the others were placed with various family members. And not the grandparents, yet they want your daughter."

They probably just want her checks, he thought uncharitably. All this time and he had no idea of his daughter's family or situation. Pam's mom's arrogance and her father's lack of interest for their other grandkids disgusted him. He should have checked, pushed for visitation, something.

"It doesn't matter. Proceed with the case. If we have to go to court, so be it. And Brian—"

"Yeah?"

"You need to win this one. It was one thing letting her live with her mom. Now, she comes with me. Family. Got that?"

Cherise had been right about that. He was responsible and he'd no longer pass her off to others. Whatever it took, he'd do right by his child.

"Got it, my man."

"Good, later."

Chapter 13

The two-story beige brick building seemed cold and unwelcoming. Ross found it hard to believe this place housed Family Services when it looked so blah. Inside, the block walls had been painted beige and held random announcement posters. This agency held his daughter. A quick glance showed two manila folders in his hand. One had the distressing report from his business. Someone was stealing and messing with their bottom line. The other folder had all the data and legal information about Lenora, his five-year-old daughter.

He placed the work file inside his book bag and signed in. Later, he looked through the glass at the small child sitting unresponsive at the desk in the middle of the room. The counselor held up various objects while talking to her. Yet she remained silent. He watched as the counselor showed her pictures of animals, buildings, people and then her mother. She became animated.

"Mommy, where's mommy?" Lenora's small voice asked anxiously. Her voice had a whiny, grainy quality. He listened as the counselor talked about her mother and showed her a picture of her with her siblings and their mother.

"That's Sammy, Fee-fee, Mommy and Nora," she said grabbing the picture and hugging it with a light laugh.

Her joy sparked something deep within him. Standing still, he took a serious look at his daughter, the product of a drunken debacle. Seeing her now, no

Erosa Knowles- Men of 3X CONStruction
Book 1

paternity test was required. Lenora was his own mini-me.

Her long thick ponytail, a myriad of hues of browns, hung to the middle of her back. Wayward curls escaped and framed an angular face, similar to his, with high cheeks and straight nose. He couldn't see her eyes from this position, but he knew her eyes were hazel, twins to his own.

He'd been in meetings all week with medical professionals, and Social Services. There was no question, he was next in line for custody, but all the parties involved wanted to make sure he understood the magnitude of the task he'd be undertaking.

In reality, he had no clue and asked for all the help they were willing to give him. He sat stunned at the amount of information. Each professional who worked with Lenora praised her mom for the great care she'd provided. His conscience lightened knowing she'd had good care in a loving home.

The first thing he needed was a live-in housekeeper and a nearby school for her, since she'd be moving. Ms. Connie worked on a housekeeper for him. He hated she spent more time out of the office, but she assured him Cathy had a handle on things.

Initially, he suspected she dragged her feet locating help for his house; perhaps waiting for Cherise to appear and save the day. All that changed when the older woman met Lenora. He watched the meeting through the glass. His daughter didn't stand a chance against Ms. Connie's loving. By the end of the interview, Lenora stood near the older woman, although she never uttered a word.

Inhaling, he mentally prepared himself for anything

and headed for the door. He'd been warned it might take a while for her to attach to him.

Two light brown eyes looked in his direction and then slid to the side of the room when he walked in.

"Hello," he said, watching her.

"Hello," the counselor replied, glancing at him before looking at Lenora, who turned away, grasping the picture of her family.

"Lenora, would you like to meet Ross. He came to meet you; he was a friend of your mama."

Ross tensed at the lie, but realized it may be the only way to get Lenora to pay him any attention.

"Hi Lenora, can I see the pretty picture of your mommy and brothers?" he asked moving in her direction.

"Fee-fee is not my brother, she's my sister." Her eyes glanced over at him and back to the picture again.

"Oh, okay. Is your sister as pretty as you? No, I don't think so. What do you think?" He'd been told she was extremely smart and quite literal. He hoped he hadn't asked too many questions.

Her brow furrowed before she answered him. "She is my sister, so yes, she is as pretty as I am. Have you seen her?" Her eyes looked above his head as she held the picture in front of her, so he could see.

"Ahh, you're right."

She laughed and pulled the picture to her chest. He glanced at the counselor who smiled and nodded. Assuming it was encouragement for him to continue, he licked dry lips, and glanced at his palm where he'd written cues from her teacher about the things she liked to talk about.

"Can you swim?"

Her head whipped around, a large smile creased her face. "Yes! Yes! I can swim. Mommy took Fee-fee and me to the pool. I'm a good swimmer." She placed one arm in front of her, pulled it back and then the other. Her neck swiveled from side to side as she blew out air. "See…I can swim."

He laughed at her antics, and she continued, becoming more energetic. His daughter was a ham. Beautiful, when she smiled it was if an inner bulb went off inside her. He sat on the floor not too far from her chair and relaxed.

He caught the tail end of the conversation between the counselor and his daughter. She became demanding and stubborn until she turned in his direction and glared at him.

"Mommy showed me your picture, why won't you take me home. I want to go home! I want to go home!" She stomped her foot and threw a book down.

"Pick up that book, Lenora," he said before thinking.

She pouted, picked it up, and placed it on the table. Marching to a chair, she sat and turned her back to both adults.

"What the hell?" he mouthed to the counselor, who shrugged. Stumped, he didn't know what to do. No one factored in that she may have a clue to his identity. What had Pam told her? He knew his name was on the birth certificate and Lenora had his last name. But what else?

"Lenora, when did mommy show you my picture? What did she tell you about me?" He gentled his voice.

He hadn't meant to snap at her, but the counselor smiled and nodded at him when he did it. She seemed to be doing a lot of that.

"Did Mommy tell you I was pretty, is that why she showed you my picture?" He picked at some imaginary lint on his pants, feeling her gaze on him.

"No! You're not pretty. Girls are pretty, boys are handsome. Mommy said so."

"Ahhhh," he said nodding his head. He waited. It didn't take long.

"Mommy said you're my daddy. Mommy said you were coming to pick me up, and I had to be a big girl and go with my daddy." The matter of fact tone of voice shocked him. She could've been reading the Harry Potter book on the table.

He glanced towards the two-way glass, surely, someone was there who could clue him on what to do, what to say at this point. No one had told his daughter her mother would never be coming back, and he wasn't scheduled to take her home for a few more days. The brilliant professionals thought it would take that long for her to accept him in her life.

"How did you feel about that?" He asked, feeling his way. "Me picking you up and taking you with me?" He needed to know what he was dealing with here. Although she talked to him, did that mean she understood?

"Okay. Allie my friend at school has a daddy. He's littler than you, though." She played with some sort of movable cube.

"Oh yeah?" He didn't know what to say after that

remark.

"Her daddy picks her up from school and takes her for ice cream and McDonald's." Her tawny eyes slid over him, while her lips turned upward at the corners. He'd swear the sun broke through the walls and shone just for them.

"That sounds about right."

"You never took me to McDonalds." She faced him squarely, hands on her waist, face scrunched.

He laughed at her posturing. She stared, before smiling and jumped on him. "You can't laugh at me, Daddy. You have to take me to McDonalds."

"I can do that." He squeezed her tight before releasing her. His throat worked as a knot formed, choking his words. Warmth bathed him as she smiled at him, acceptance freely given. His heart raced and soared at the kind reception in her eyes. Why couldn't everything be as uncomplicated as a child's adoration and approval?

Chapter 14

Cherise's nail's scratched the armrest of the seat. She tried to appear calm as the plane rose higher. Her stomach clenched as she rejected various scenarios of her impending reunion with Ross. The breathing exercises hadn't helped. Nothing had. One minute, she was scared he'd lost interest, and excited of his heated response the next.

"This is stupid," she muttered, disgusted over how worked up she'd gotten. Crossing her legs, she closed her eyes. She'd been nervous, but determined to correct things with him.

Her plan had been simple. Call, see how he was doing and then apologize. He'd been wrong for not telling her about his child. But she never should have hung up and shut down when he didn't agree with her. She'd been wrong for that.

Simple—short and sweet, right? Wrong. Ross wouldn't even discuss the matter on the phone. She replayed the conversation in her mind.

"Hi, Ross. It's me, Cherise."

"Hey, when did you get back?" His voice, deep and smoky, touched places in her only he could reach.

"Earlier today." She heard some noise in the background.

"When are you coming back?"

"I'm not sure. I thought I'd get—"

"There will be a ticket waiting for you at the airport

tomorrow. I'll call you back with the time. Don't unpack, if you already have, leave it or repack it. But be on the flight tomorrow."

She'd been stunned by his demand. When he asked if she understood, she'd simply said yes. Her carefully practiced speech discarded, unused. The emotions she'd held in check all week were all over the place.

Happy he wanted her, confused he wouldn't talk about their problems, disappointed he hadn't begged her forgiveness and uncertain about his relationship with his child. Her mom thought he handled the situation just right and made sure she didn't miss the flight, which left twelve hours after the call. The man worked fast.

Now, doubts assailed her. The conversation had been too brief for her to determine if he was angry. He flat out refused to discuss anything over the phone. So, here she sat. Miles high in the air, on her way to see her man. She clenched her fist as she prayed he was still hers.

"Honey, are you all right?"

Reluctantly, Cherise opened her eyes and looked into glazed emerald green ones seated next to her. Oh shit, she's drunk. Swallowing, she nodded. "I'm fine."

"First time?"

"No, just got a lot on my mind."

"Hmmm, don't we all." The platinum blonde lifted her glass, threw back the contents, and then patted her lips with the napkin. "Don't let him get to you. Men are all assholes. That's why we have to screw them." The stranger chuckled at her own wit.

Cherise turned away and looked down the aisle. Hopefully, there was another empty seat. Every damn seat in first class was taken. She wasn't mad enough to move to coach.

She grimaced as the woman tapped her arm. "Yes?" Invasion of her personal space still bothered her.

"Could you wave at that flight attendant there? My glass is empty."

Cherise glanced upward at the call button and then back at the fake Barbie. Her mother's training kept her from snapping her irritation. "Sure, no problem." She waved at the attendant, and leaned back when he approached their row.

After, her seatmate ordered another cocktail, Cherise attempted to relax again by replaying images of her last time with Ross. It had been two days before graduation. The two of them had been at her apartment, watching a movie. Halfway through, she decided she wanted to play. Ross wanted to finish the movie. She grinned remembering how she got him to change his mind. Her hand rubbed his cock, he moaned and widened his legs. She dropped to the floor between them. The sounds he made excited her, and then—

"You spend a lot of time in Detroit?"

Didn't people understand boundaries? If a person's eyes were closed, that meant they were unavailable. Cherise ignored the question and the speaker.

The infuriating woman tapped her arm. "I'm just visiting Detroit, I was wondering if you knew of a good place to party. I plan on being there for a week."

"No, I don't know Detroit. I'm meeting a friend." Her prayer that the short answer would squelch the conversation went unanswered.

"Oh. Boyfriend? Girlfriend?"

Without opening her eyes, Cherise snapped, "Neither."

###

The suitcase seemed harder to pull with each step Cherise took up the jetway. She glanced around the boarding area for Ross and remembered he couldn't access this area without a boarding pass. Breathing a sigh of relief, she headed out to the concourse.

Her seatmate caught up, chatting as only the inebriated could. Cherise had no idea what the woman talked about, and realized it didn't matter. The woman was prone to carrying on a one-sided conversation.

"Hot damn," the woman said stopping. "Now that's a man."

Since she'd ceased movement right in front of her, Cherise had no choice but to stop. She looked in the direction the woman stared.

Her mouth went dry watching Ross look at the arrival board and then head in her direction. Belatedly, she noticed other women, and a couple of men, watched his long strides through the congested corridor. Sunglasses covered his eyes, but she remembered their intensity when he focused. He zeroed in on her gate number.

She knew the moment he saw her staring. He smiled. A tremor shook her. She swallowed before she drooled. He looked that good in his snug jeans and short-sleeved shirt. Her nipples hardened in need. He always had this impact on her and it blew her away. Her body recognized him and craved his touch.

One foot moved in front of the other. Pretty soon they were face to face. His damn sunglasses kept her from reading him, but before she could utter a word, he grabbed her to his chest. Her carryon hit the ground as he squeezed her tight.

"Baby, I missed you," he moaned, right before he kissed her.

Time halted. His arms offered sanctuary, soothed her tattered nerves. His mouth, warm and sweet, sent her mind reeling. Her womb clenched as moisture flooded her panties. Her body let him know how much she missed him. Reluctantly, he drew back. Looked at her and stole a peck on her lips.

"I missed you, too," she said as she rubbed his arm. More to maintain contact, assure herself he was there than anything else. She'd been dreaming of him every day; the reality of his arms much better than her imagination. Her heart overflowed with emotion as he pulled her tight again.

He bent to pick up her luggage and frowned at the blonde staring at them.

The woman walked over as Cherise turned in her direction. "Sweetie, forget everything I said about men on the plane. They don't make'em like this anymore. Damn, to have a man who don't give a damn about anything or anybody else… shit the way he kissed you just then. Now that's the real fucking deal." She squealed and walked off.

Ross leaned close. "Do I want to know?" He asked, tilting his head at the woman's back.

Erosa Knowles- Men of 3X CONStruction
Book 1

"No. I sat next to her on the plane. She's drunk."

He squeezed her waist. "You have more luggage?"

"No," she said, looking at him.

"Good, let's get out of here so I can greet you right."

Cherise nodded, too full of emotion to speak. The questions or doubts of him wanting her vanished. His hard cock had given her a personal welcome. Being with him again was mind-blowing. She'd behaved like a child having a temper tantrum and he'd welcomed her with wide arms.

She'd made the mistake and mentioned to her mother that she hadn't told Ross about her anxiety disorder or therapy or her battle to stay in control. The rebuke she'd received as well as the hypocrisy of her actions with Ross sent her into a deep funk. She'd make things right and come clean. She loved him and hoped he'd forgive her.

He placed his hand on the small of her back and walked towards the parking garage.

"Hungry?" he asked into the silence.

"Not much. I could eat something."

Ross nodded as he pulled out his keys and punched a button. The trunk lifted on his car. He walked to the passenger side and opened the door. After placing the luggage beside his in the trunk, he walked to the driver's side, slid in and pulled her close. Her mouth tasted of mint and Coke. He stroked her inner recesses and tangled with her tongue. She pulled his head closer, tugging his hair. He felt something wet on his face and pulled away.

Leaning forward he kissed away the salty fluid. "Cherise, baby, what's the matter?" he murmured.

Her hands touched his face, smoothed his lips while

she cried harder. Loud sobs wracked her body as her head fell to his shoulder.

His hands rubbed her back. "What's wrong?" His heart boomed in his chest at her distress. Something major had her upset. Pain stabbed at him, he needed to make this better for her.

"I...I messed up. I left when you...you needed me the most. I'm sorry, Ross. I'm so sorry."

"Shhhhh, it's okay, baby. Don't cry, it's okay." The tension eased from his chest. It still hurt to see her upset, but he could work with this. They'd work it out.

"No, it's not!" She sobbed. "I messed up. I ran off like a child."

At the time, her abandoning him pierced his soul. Over the past week, spending time with Nora, as she preferred to be called, he accepted his responsibility. He needed to bond with his child; they'd needed that time alone together to strengthen their relationship. Everything had worked out for the best. Now they needed to heal this relationship. It was just as important to him.

A whirring sound filled the car. He moved backwards. "Hold up, baby," he whispered.

Head down, she moved back. Ross lifted her from her seat and placed her on his lap. Her head rested on his chest. The tears continued to flow. He stroked her back.

"I really like you a lot, Ross," she confessed. "I thought about you every day, how I talked to you. What you said, how you sounded. I put myself in your shoes." She sighed. "You had been through some terrible mess. And then I tripped on you. God, I hate I did that."

He rubbed her back, making soothing sounds, allowing her to get everything out of her system.

"Please forgive me. I know I do selfish stuff sometimes, but I want us to make this work."

"Baby, it's forgotten. You weren't the only one doing some thinking. I messed up, too. I'm not used to explaining anything. And since I had no in-your-face relationship with Lenora, I simply didn't think about having a kid." He sighed. "It never occurred to me to tell you about her." Shame pierced his heart now that he had a chance to spend time with his baby girl. How could he have forgotten his child? What kind of self-centered bastard did that make him? Knowing he'd been contentedly living his life, uninvolved with Lenora hurt like hell.

Cherise bit his chest through his shirt.

"Hey, cut that out. Don't start nothing. We won't make it to the hotel."

She looked up at him. "Hotel?"

He nodded and kissed her forehead. "Yeah, I'm kidnapping you for a couple of days. My intention was for us to have this conversation later, much later. After we kick it a bit. But it's all good. Whatever you need."

"I need you," she said before kissing his chest.

"I need you more. You have no idea how much I missed you. Are you feeling better?"

She nodded and returned to her seat.

Ross started the car, leaned forward and kissed her again. His thumb wiped across her face while his eyes searched hers. He nodded. She looked good. Just having her in his arms again soothed something within him.

Nothing was settled between them. But the pulsing need to have her with him rested.

He'd demanded, almost ordered her to his side, pushing the travel agent to get her to Michigan as soon as possible. God had answered his prayers. His woman was back in his life and wanted to be with him.

The room he'd booked for them was in a resort outside the city. Ms. Connie had Lenora and wholeheartedly agreed with his plan to spend some time alone with Cherise. Reaching out, he grabbed her hand and held on. Pleased when she threaded their fingers together. It didn't escape his notice she never asked where they were going.

His battered heart flipped with pride knowing she trusted him, in this at least. Her finger ran over the back of his hand. Goosebumps exploded over his overheated flesh. He barely contained the shudder that threatened.

"What are you up to?" he asked.

"Nothing, just loving the contrast. Your hands, they're hard with calluses. Right here," she rubbed the back of his hand softly, "they're soft."

"I work hard for a living." He squeezed her hand.

"I know. I like that. I like you."

His heart stuttered. Exhaling, he hoped he spoke in a calm tone that wouldn't betray how far gone he was over her. "I like you more."

"Impossible," she whispered before nipping the tip of his finger with her teeth.

The tremor whipped through him so fast, he hadn't a hope of stopping it. Fuck it, she played with fire, she'd

Erosa Knowles- Men of 3X CONStruction
Book 1

know his heat. "I'm close to the edge, baby. Don't play with me like this. My woman has been AWOL and I ain't had no loving since she left me." His tone became gruff, hoarse with need.

"Hmpf," she said. "She shouldn't have done that. I bet she's in pretty bad shape herself. I mean what woman in her right mind would walk away from this?" The flat of her hand rested on the juncture between his legs.

His cocked jumped and rose at the contact. He groaned. "Do not."

"What?" she asked as her hand lifted and fell.

He inhaled and looked around the highway. There was no place to pull over, traffic was thick. They had at least another thirty minutes before reaching the resort. It was too far. Whose idea was it anyway to stay between Detroit and Lapeer? There was nothing for it. He had to bring himself under control.

"Baby, how was the graduation?" He asked to get her mind off setting his body on fire. Any respite would help.

"Fine."

"That's it? Fine? Are you still angry I missed it?" *Thank God she stopped touching. Now if he could get it to soften just a bit. Hell, not happening.*

"What? No!" Her voice rose. "I mean, I wanted you there to share with me. Show you off to my mom. Who wants to meet you, by the way."

He nodded, hoping he hadn't missed anything she'd said.

"It's just, well, that moment will never come again." Her voice dropped as she removed her hand from his crotch.

Well, damn! He wanted to end the torment, but not head into those waters. "I know, baby," he murmured. "I planned on being there with you. I bragged to my boys and everything. I'm sorry."

She patted his hand and lapsed into silence. He pushed a button and soft jazz played. Hopefully, the soft sounds would neutralize the sexually charged atmosphere in the car. Out of the corner of his eye, he saw her press another button. A classic rhythm and blues radio station. He swallowed as her hand, that evil instrument, tapped in tune with an O'Jays song on his thigh.

He looked at the road marker; another ten minutes and they should be there. Sweat broke out on his forehead as he tried to think of something, anything disgusting to counter the raging desire assaulting him as she scraped her nails along his inner thigh.

In a desperate move, he grabbed her hand and held it still on his leg. *What the fuck?* Who was Teddy Pendergrass? How did Cherise know this song? He listened as she sang, "come on and go with me." She smiled as another song by the same man came on.

"Ohhh, It so good loving somebody!" She clapped her hands and sang along. "I love his music, don't you?" She asked as he pulled into the resort.

"Yeah, uh-huh. Sounds good." He needed to get his l'il man down to a decent level or the valet would see more than he wanted him to.

"They don't make music like that anymore. I mean, a lot of the rap music I don't understand."

That comment bought him up short. Not understand

rap? Where had she been? "You don't like rap?"

She rolled her eyes at him while straightening her dress. "Not all black people like rap. And I didn't say I didn't like it. I said I don't understand all of it."

He eased behind the car in front, popped the trunk and waited for the valet. For some reason, her comments were distracting enough. His boner was no longer an issue.

That lasted until the elevator when she leaned into him. And he was back, heavy and aching. He grabbed her to him, greedy for another taste of her sweetness. God, he'd missed this. The weeks leading to her graduation, they'd lived together. Slept every night and woke every morning in the same bed. He missed that closeness.

He allowed her to enter the suite first, more to watch her ass swish in that dress she wore, teasing him out of his mind. His temptress thought they might've been over. No fucking way. No matter what, they'd work everything out. Right now, he needed her.

"Come here." Playtime was over.

She turned from peeking in a door. He stood in front of the sofa. He watched her saunter over to him, a smile on her face.

"Undress me."

Her breath hitched as her hands moved toward his belt. The temperature in the room rose as she licked her lips while unsnapping his jeans. One hand pulled the zipper down, while the other held the back of his ass.

She was enjoying this.

He was in hell. Her head brushed his cock as she bent, pulling his jeans down.

"Oops, forgot your shoes," she muttered.

He kicked them off. Hell, he'd do anything to get them where he wanted them to be—naked in bed.

"Thanks, baby," she murmured before she kissed his calf and rubbed her face against it.

"Finish it." Tiny tremors shot through his body.

"Okay, okay. It's just I miss you."

"You're going to get me."

Laughing, she pulled his shirt up, exposing his abs and chest. "Baby, I just have to," she murmured before kissing his stomach.

This was the worse idea he'd ever had. He'd lost control over the situation. He snatched the shirt over his head, her mouth latched onto his nipple.

His body shook with desire.

Grabbing her waist, he marched in the direction of the bedroom and tossed her on the bed.

"You have one second to get out of that dress if you want to keep it," he ground out while pulling off his boxers.

A small smile lit the corner of his face as she scrambled pulling the offending garment over her head. Her bra fell next. He dove onto the bed and pulled her under him. Her arms wrapped around him. His fingers trust into her hot core as his lips suckled her tight nipples. She bucked and he added a finger and deepened the thrusts.

Oh God, she was so tight and hot. He wouldn't be able to wait. He needed her now. "Sorry," he whispered. His fingers pulled out and he slid home. He let his cock rest snug in its customized sheath, and savoring her slight tremors.

"Move, Ross, please," she wailed, her hands slapping his ass.

He lifted out to the tip, gazed at the passion in her eyes, and slammed home. Her sigh of pleasure spurred him forward. His mind allowed his body to take them to a place where the only thing he comprehended was pleasure. Deeper, harder, he pulled her legs over his elbows and pistoned hard and deep. His back worked to reach it, to give her the ultimate release. His balls tightened, he felt her spasm and scream her release. He kept stroking, faster, higher.

"Oh shit, oh shit," he yelled as he pumped into her. He felt it from his toes. He couldn't stop. He heard her yell as her pussy grasped and tightened again.

He exploded. Spots leapt before his eyes. Sweat poured off him. Messy sex, he loved it. In a moment, he'd be able to breathe again.

"Baby?"

"Hmmm?" he answered, veering to the side to move off her, only to be feel her tighten her hands on his ass.

"Don't move and you can be sorry anytime you want."

It took a moment for him to understand her comment. He smiled. "You got it." He kissed the top of her head. She sang the song from the car, her voice was whispery soft. Her hips moved, offering herself.

He rolled over and gazed into her eyes.

She leaned up and took a kiss. He groaned. They were still connected and he was hardening inside her unbelievably fast.

"Love it like this," she whispered.

Her words penetrated his lust-filled brain. She did something inside that squeezed his hardening cock. His breath caught. She was killing him.

"So good...so good," she sang. Her eyes were half closed, but she watched him.

He watched her. There were serious undercurrents going on here. He recognized and appreciated them. It felt good to know he wasn't alone in his feelings.

"Love me then," he whispered, leading the charge. He surged upward, holding her hips, ensuring she took him.

She threw her head back and moaned, loud and long.

He hardened more.

Placing her hands on each side of his head, she stared into his eyes as he slammed down. "I do," she murmured.

He felt her tense and shiver. Her tremors always excited him. They signaled her pleasure, her release. It was his job to *know* she experienced ultimate pleasure.

Chapter 15

Cherise's head lay on Ross's chest. She inhaled as aftershocks ran through her body. This was a good idea. If nothing else, her memory from tonight would feed her for months. Tonight she'd tell him. Her heart stuttered at the thought and her breath hitched.

"Better?"

"Much. I was just thinking this was a great idea. I needed this. Just you."

"We needed this. I need you," his voice soft near her ear.

Her heart jumped. What was he saying? She moved to the side. Their bodies made noises at the separation. She looked up at him and they laughed. "Shower," she said and rolled off the bed.

Later, after playing in the Jacuzzi, they sat at the table eating room service. Her stomach roiled, she pushed the food around on the plate. So many things needed sorting out: their relationship, living arrangements, his daughter, her job prospects. Ross looked relaxed, at peace. She never wanted that to change, but it would.

He looked at his watch. "Nora came home with me a couple of days ago. Ms. Connie has been helping me with her while I try to find a housekeeper. Would I be offending her if I called to check to see how things are going?"

Cherise shook her head. "Ms. Connie thinks you hung the sun. You couldn't offend her. I think she'd be disappointed if you didn't call. Trust me, she thinks very highly of you."

He stared at her for a moment and then took out his cell, punched a number and waited. Jealousy flashed through her. It was petty and a wasted emotion. Another woman had given him a child. The child had just lost her mama, probably the one staple in her life.

She'd put the plans she and Ross had made to live together after her graduation on hold for a few months. Or until Nora became accustomed to him and her new living arrangements. She quelled the disappointment that rose inside. It might be tough at first. Perhaps she could get an apartment nearby. Actually, she should get a place near her job. They could see each other on the weekends.

"Cherise!" Ross snapped, bringing her out of her mental ramblings.

"What?"

"I said Ms. Connie said to tell you hi."

"Oh…all right. Tell her hi."

He gazed at her and then glanced at his closed phone. "What were you thinking about so hard?"

"Does she look like you?"

He glanced at her. "She's my mini-me." He laughed at her frown. "Austin Powers, mini-me, get it?"

She shook her head, trying to find the relevance.

"Yeah, baby, she looks like me."

He reached across the table and took her hand. "She's my daughter. I didn't watch her grow to this point. I never saw her face until this past week. I should've fought for my rights while her mama was alive. I didn't. I missed time with her I'll never get back. You were right; she's my family, my responsibility. Thanks for being my rock and setting me straight, even when I didn't want to hear it."

There it was, her opening. "No problem. I'm glad you stepped up to the plate and got your house in order so to speak. I want to meet her later. We have to make sure she doesn't get overwhelmed with all the new people in her life. Did she have brothers and sisters?"

He nodded.

"Will she be able to see them?"

"I doubt it. They split them up between relatives. I was the only one to get my kid."

Slipping into professional mode, she nodded. "Okay, so that means she has no one from her old life. After I'm settled, I want to help you with her. She sounds smart, and if she's your twin, I'm sure she's a handful."

"She is a handful, but you'll know that since you'll be sleeping down the hall from her." His voice carried a steel undertone.

She knew this wouldn't be easy. "Ross, do you think that's a good idea? The two of you just met. Why not wait until things are solid before you introduce me to her?"

"No."

"No?"

"How about, hell no."

She closed her eyes. The selfish part of her rejoiced, did a little hoopla dance. The noble part of her scolded and insisted she do what was best for the child. "Ross—"

"Look at me, Cherise," he snapped. The relaxed man of the past hour disappeared. In his place sat an implacable man who wouldn't accept her answer.

Thank you, God! How far was she willing to take the noble train anyway? Each child was different. While she'd never be the child's birth mother, she could be her friend.

She locked eyes with him.

"No one, and I mean no one, dictates my life to me. If you don't want to be with me, say so. No games. We agreed to move in together after your graduation. Well, you graduated. I will regret to my death that I missed it. But that can't be changed. If we are to continue this relationship, we will be together. In every way. That is not up for debate. My daughter will adapt and adjust. We all will."

His games comment stung a little. But her mom had called her out on it before. Being noble wasn't as important as she'd thought. She loved him and that made it easy to give in.

"I love you, Ross."

"I know and I love you, too. But that does not mean I'm going to play around with this. It's my life and I need to know where you stand."

Her heart jumped at his declaration. She stood and walked around the table, blinking back tears. Her hand cupped his face.

"Aww, don't start crying, Cherise. You can't do that every time we have a serious discussion. I'm—"

She shut him up with a kiss. He pulled her onto his lap, deepening their passion. *Mine*, the word flitted through her mind.

"I love you," she purred the moment he let her up for

Erosa Knowles- Men of 3X CONStruction
Book 1

air.

"I love you more," he panted and kissed her again.
###

Later that night, Cherise tried getting comfortable,
but couldn't. Guilt rode her hard. She hadn't trusted
Ross's love enough to come clean about her medical
condition. Shame merged with the taint of hypocrisy until
nausea and vertigo shook her frame.

She would lose him for sure.

The certainty of the loss tilted her world and knocked
her into the abyss of anxiety. Caught in the grip of
paralyzing fear, she fought to hold tight to his declarations
of love, but her deception blocked her ability to believe.
How could he really love her when he didn't know of her
disorder? That changed everything. His love was built on
the sands of a lie.

He walked in naked and caught her shivering. Any
minute and he'd see what she'd desperately tried to hide.
The loving concern in his hazel eyes pierced her heart.
Her body jerked.

Tears pooled in her eyes as the look of horror crossed
his face. Her heart stuttered and then galloped as she
struggled to harness air. Pain exploded across her head as
she dropped to her knees, shaking uncontrollably.

"Cherise," Ross called her name and ran off.

Her greatest fear had come true. Random thoughts
flew through her mind, slips of information, answers to
questions; useless in the face of trauma. The searing pain
in her chest reinforced the notion of death. Her limbs
ached. She moaned in agony.

Ross knew her secret and left. She'd gambled and

lost.

You're not dying. This is just an attack. Fight through it.

The words floated in the back of her mind, she shook them off. They echoed again, this time she tried to pay attention through the pain.

Hands pulled her head down, the nausea slowed. "You'll be okay, help will be here soon. Breathe slowly. Take your time, love. Just breathe, don't leave me, Cherise. I love you."

Through the hellish fog, she heard Ross's voice. He hadn't left her. She tried to show him how much that meant to her, but the darkness took her first.

###

Cherise blinked opened her eyes. Confused, she glanced at the circular curtain. Her hand opened and touched the hard bed. Inhaling, she closed her eyes.

Hospital.

Her heart sank, two years she'd gone without an attack and then wham. She covered her face with her free arm.

"Hey, welcome back, baby," Ross said, entering the small curtained area. "You scared the hell out of me."

Her tongue felt fat and stuck to the roof of her mouth. She nodded in misery and shame.

He touched her forehead. "You need anything? I can call the nurse."

She shook her head frantically, and croaked. "No."

"Okay, calm down." He stared at her.

She turned her head to the side in shame.

Erosa Knowles- Men of 3X CONStruction
Book 1

"I met your mama."

Cherise closed her eyes, humiliated. Her mom had been headed to Michigan for a conference. They'd left for the airport together. It wouldn't have taken her any time to reach the hospital.

"Do you want me to get her?" Ross sounded out of his depth. She took pity on him and nodded.

"Okay, I'll be right back." He left the room quietly.

She pushed the button to raise the head of the bed and took the cup on the table next to the bed. Glad it was water, she drank, soothing her tongue and throat.

"Hi, baby girl," a subdued Veronique said walking in the room, Ross right behind her.

"Hi, Mama." She sent Ross a wan smile. "You met Ross?"

"Yeah, he answered your phone as the ambulance was putting you in the back. I've been here about an hour." She sat and pushed strands of hair from around Cherise's face. "You okay?"

"I don't know yet." She glanced at a silent Ross. "Am I?"

"As far as I know, you had a panic attack. A bad one. The symptoms resembled a heart attack, that's what scared me so bad, but pass within twenty to thirty minutes. It shouldn't have lasted as long as yours did. They had your records on file and were able to stabilize you quickly." He rattled off the information with surgical precision.

She closed her eyes. The coolness of her mother's palm touched her face. She leaned down and kissed her cheek.

Cherise met her calm gaze.

Her mom winked. "Ross, you have things under control here." She smiled in his direction. "Call me after you move and get settled, Cherise. I'm meeting your dad next week; I want to be able to give him a good report." She looked at Ross when she said the last.

Move, get settled? Her mama must have misread the signals. Ross wouldn't have her moving in with him, not after finding out about her problem.

"Will do, Veronique," Ross said into the silence.

Her mama nodded, kissed her cheek again and left the room.

The silence screamed to be filled. Her fascination with the opposite side of the room was a cop out. She needed to face him. Slowly, she turned. Ross sat reading a document of some sort. His furrowed brow made her curious.

"What's that?" she whispered.

"This?" he looked at her. "This is background information on Generalized Anxiety Disorders. Your mom gave it to me." He glanced at her and then continued reading.

"I'm sorry."

"Sorry? What for?"

"Sorry for not telling you about my disorder."

"Why should you have told me, Cherise?"

She frowned. This conversation sounded familiar. "So you could decide if you wanted to be with a woman with mental challenges." She swallowed her shame as the conversation from the restaurant returned full force.

Erosa Knowles- Men of 3X CONStruction
Book 1

"According to this, and everything the doctors say, your condition is containable. It was set off by some events or an event. After a year of training, you should be fine. Your mom said you haven't had an attack for over two years."

She nodded.

"I don't embarrass easy, but your mom had me hanging on by a thread demanding to know what we'd been doing that caused this attack." He kneeled beside the bed. "Was it something we did that bought this on. I've wracked my brain and there was nothing we hadn't done before."

"No, it wasn't you." She swallowed as tears pooled in her eyes. "It was the guilt eating at me for not being honest, yet demanding honesty from you. Falling in love and deceiving you twisted me up inside. I wanted to tell you, but the fear choked me. It grew bigger in my mind to the point I couldn't handle it anymore."

"You had attacks before, didn't you? A few times, you got sick, I put your head down and it got better. That didn't work this time."

"No, it was too late. The fear had grown too big."

"Fear? Fear of what? " Ross asked, sounding genuinely confused. "I don't understand what you were afraid of." The pad of his thumb touched her cheek and came away wet.

"Having panic attacks isn't all there is to the disorder. It's also the lengths you go through to avoid the attacks. That behavior runs your life." She waved down his question and stared at him.

"I was scared shitless of your reaction to learning

about my disorder. I saw it as a mental disease and all the baggage that comes with that label. It wasn't a visitor, it couldn't be expunged like your record, I feel the stain of it every day of my life. I thought it was bad, so of course you'd see it the same way." She looked away. "I was positive of your negative reaction to my problem and that led to avoiding telling you the truth, which fed the fear of your finding out. I thought I had beaten the disorder; instead, I brought in a new demon to feed it, the terror of losing you."

"I'm still here." He bent and kissed her lips. "I wished you'd have talked to me instead of punishing yourself."

"Me, too." What else could she say? He'd seen her at her worse and was still here. She breathed easier. "When can I go home?"

"They want to keep you overnight, but we can leave in the morning." He winked and stood. "You thirsty? Hungry?"

She coughed. "Aren't you mad at me for not telling you?"

"I was too scared of losing you to be mad. All I could think was I can't lose her now, not after all we'd been through. I made all kinds of promises to the big guy upstairs for you to come through." He brushed her lips and stroked her face.

"Can you still love me, knowing I'm damaged?" she whispered her biggest fear.

Ross picked up her hand and kissed her palm. "It's hard letting others see past your face into your baggage aint it? When is the right time to tell someone your darkest fears, huh? How do you know who to trust with parts of your soul?" His lips brushed hers.

She smiled against his lips as he repeated some of the questions from a previous discussion. She gave the same answer. "I don't know."

"We've been through a lot and most of it could've been avoided if we'd trusted each other and opened up about our past. How can I be mad at you when I refused to let you see my dark places? If anybody can understand your fear, it's me," he said. His thumb ran over his lip.

She bit down gently.

"One question though, is that why you have boxes of pencils?"

She groaned. "In a way. I've always needed to write with sharp leads."

"Is that also the reason you overanalyze everything?"

She nodded. Obviously he'd noticed more than she thought and hadn't said anything.

"I can live with it." He bent forward and gave her a long lip-locking kiss.

Chapter 16

The temperature in his office was moderate, but a cold chill crept up Ross's spine. His mind numb, as if he'd tossed back excessive amounts of Grey Goose. Wispy images of construction jobs they'd completed hovered around the edges of his memory. No matter how hard he tried, the items in front of him did not match the jobs.

Not good.

Mentally, he tabulated the time and energy it would take to fix yet another problem. This situation warranted the involvement of all three of them, which might cause a slow down on the Big Lakes site. Contracts needed fulfillment, obligations met, and bills paid.

Once again, he questioned his desire for ownership. The administrative difficulties drained, and prevented him from working with his hands as he craved. This new problem was simple and complicated.

His eyes darted to the door, a sense of foreboding wrapped around his chest and squeezed. Red and Smoke moved towards the vacant chairs in Ross's office and sat quietly. Red's nostrils pinched in obvious preparation for a confrontation. Smoke sat and watched, first Cathy who sat in front of the desk, and then at Ross. He nodded at them and glanced at the paper clenched in his hand.

Cathy placed a stack of papers on his desk. Her smile did not quite reach her eyes. Ross placed the paper he held on his desk and looked across the room at his certifications hanging on the wall. They were small slips of paper signifying his time, money and energy, slices of his life to reach a certain goal.

Someone took a shortcut, no respect given to what he and his partners worked and achieved. That crap would not fly, not with him, not with his partners and not with his crew. Heat rose up his neck. His lips stretched taut like a newly-tuned guitar string, two of his fingers tapped the sheet of paper that heralded the damning information.

His stomach clenched as shards of pain mixed with a heavy dose of anger, coaxed the remnants of his breakfast to the surface. He swallowed the rage, tamped it back, determined to maintain control. Tightened fists echoed the demand to his nerves to settle, he needed to think.

"Bad news?" Smoke asked after a lengthy silence.

"Yes," Cathy answered. "There have been some orders and deliveries that are missing from the back."

"There has to be more than that. My boy is levitating," Red said, pointing at Ross.

"You would—"

Ross waved at her.

Her mouth snapped and she glowered at Red, before huffing out of the office.

"What's up?" Smoke leaned forward and glanced at the crumpled paper. Red sat in his chair staring at him.

"There have been orders for supplies and merchandise for jobs we don't have."

Red scoffed. "Just send it back."

"Can't, the stuff's missing. Disappeared from the back."

Smoke pivoted and looked at Red and then Ross.

"Who signed it out?"

"The paperwork has Red's initials."

"What?" Red roared. "I haven't signed out any merchandise in over two weeks. When did this happen?"

"Two, three weeks ago when you came for the pick-up for the Big Lakes project." Ross remembered that weekend clearly. He'd been next on rotation, but hadn't wanted to leave Cherise. They went to some play she wanted to see. Red had volunteered to do the pickup for him.

"Who worked inventory that week-end? Cathy?" Smoke asked.

"Yeah," Red muttered. "She had on something tight, wanted me to fuck her. But being Rubie's niece she's off limits."

Smoke and Ross nodded.

"I signed some papers just to get her out of my face. I didn't read them. Damn," he exploded. "You think she set this up?"

Smoke nodded.

Ross pursed his lips.

"What do you think, Ross?'

"I'm trying to figure out why. How's this all playing together."

"I'm listening." Red sat forward.

Smoke nodded.

"Let's go back a minute to the drugs found in Cherise's car. What if the police had found the packet? It would have been just as obvious to them as it was to me, that someone nearby put it there. All they had to do was wait to see who retrieved it."

"That's right," Red muttered.

"Wouldn't they investigate Three X Construction as well as Cherise?" Ross asked.

"Most def," Smoke said.

"And the fact we have a lot of ex-cons would have played into the media fast. No matter how I look at it, I keep thinking someone's trying to set us back. But who?" Ross sat in his chair contemplating their recent losses.

"It'd break Rubie's heart if Cathy is involved with this. We only hired her as a favor to him," Smoke said. "But I think she's mixed up some way."

"Look man, I didn't steal anything. I may have signed for the shit by accident, but I'd never steal from y'all or myself." Red yelled.

"Damn, Red, we know that. What're you doing?" Ross asked, surprised his partner thought an apology or explanation was necessary.

"That's nasty to even take it there, Red. We don't believe you'd do anything to mess up what we got going here. Chill," Smoke ordered.

Red nodded and relaxed in his chair.

"Let's have some cameras installed," Smoke said. "I hate to say this about my man Rubie's peeps, but we never had this kind of problem with just Ms. Connie. Shit's gone downhill since Cathy's working more hours."

Ross and Red nodded.

"Good idea," Ross said. "I'll set it up and personally supervise the installation. That'll keep her out of the loop."

"What's got you wired?" Smoke asked a sulking Red.

The man lived up to his nickname as his face colored. "What do you mean?"

"Just what I said. Any other time you'd blow that paperwork bullshit out your ass. Instead, you let it get to you. What's up?" Smoke asked again.

Red sighed and slumped into his chair.

"Denise," Ross answered for him, ignoring the glare Red sent his way.

"Man, you need to either step up and correct your shit, or back off and move on. You're slipping and that interferes with business." Smoke stared at the larger man while he spoke.

"Easy for you to say," Red muttered.

"What? What do you mean by that?" Smoke snarled.

Ross looked at both men. There was an underlying tension here he couldn't identify. "I've been spending a lot of time with Cherise and Nora, so obviously I'm missing something here. What's up between y'all?"

"Nothing," Red snapped.

"Nothing," Smoke said in his unflappable way.

"Nothing? Does this nothing impact Three X, in any way?" Ross demanded, pissed because they cut him out.

"How could it? It's nothing." Red smirked and stood. "I'm heading back to Big Lakes in the morning. The concrete driveway and patio stamping will be completed this week. The landscapers are almost done. We are a week and a half ahead of schedule."

Ross nodded.

"Oh, and just take the cost of the missing inventory from my check. It was sloppy of me not to check what I signed for. It won't happen again." He saluted and strutted out the door.

"Asshole," Smoke muttered.

"I heard that," Red yelled.

Ross laughed and shook his head.

###

Cherise had moved in with Ross and his daughter. The three of them settled into a truce of sorts. Lenora wanted her mother and didn't fully understand the concept or finality of death. Ross patiently explained each time she asked and never lost his temper. After a multitude of questions, Lenora accepted Cherise's presence in the house and in her daddy's bedroom. Each day Cherise learned something new about the little girl.

"What's that?" Lenora asked Cherise.

"It's a magazine about hairstyles. I'm trying a new one today."

Cherise watched out the corner of her eye as the child picked up the magazine and flipped through the pages. The child's hair reminded her of Eddie Murphy's 'Buckwheat' character, and she refused to allow anyone to touch it. She hoped Lenora's natural curiosity of some of the children's hairstyles would bring the desperately needed results. After picking up her comb, Cherise walked in front of the mirror in the master bedroom, her bedroom and began parting her hair.

Lenora followed clutching the magazine.

"I like this, my mommy used to comb my hair like this."

Cherise's heart clutched at the threadbare sound of longing in Lenora's voice. They had made progress over the past two weeks and the little girl had accepted her as much as she could although she still asked for her mom.

"Can I see?"

"It's this one." She pointed to a picture of a little girl with braids and ponytails.

It was cute and would fit her small face perfectly. "That is pretty," she said and turned back to parting her hair and braiding it.

"Do my hair like this."

Pleased that her ploy worked, Cherise hid her smile at the demand. "Okay, but I have to wash it first and then braid it. How many ponytails do you want?"

Lenora pointed at the picture. "Make it like this."

"Yes, Your Majesty," Cherise whispered as she took Lenora's hand and ushered her to the bathroom.

Chapter 17

Red looked around the Frenche property in Big Lakes. It was a beautiful work of stone and brick. He wiped his hands on the rag and pushed it further in his back pocket. The conversation he'd had yesterday with his partners nagged at him. He *was* off his game. He needed to get his head screwed on straight and focus. He didn't like feeling like the weak link. Someone deliberately set out to destroy everything the three of them built through hard work. It galled him not to lash out, or kick random asses until somebody confessed. But he had a family to care for, so he'd be cool, at least for now.

The flashing blue and white lights pulled up the driveway. Red and his crew looked up as the landscapers finished planting the shrubs near the walkway. He replaced his tee shirt and pulled his cap over his head. The concrete workers were in the back making corrections when the police arrived. Red met the officers on the porch.

He nodded. "What's up?"

"You in charge here?"

"Yes, I'm the foreman."

"We had a call that someone sold drugs from this location." One police officer looked around Red to the house.

"What?" Red said. "This is a worksite, no one lives here. My crew leaves around four o'clock every day."

"We're aware of that. But we still need to check it

out."

Red looked beyond the police officer to another car that had driven up. A K-9 unit. Great, just fucking great. "Okay, officer but I'll have to walk with you. This is an expensive home and if you break anything, the department will be replacing it."

The police officer looked askance and then nodded as the other police officers arrived and fanned out around the house. His crew backed up, giving the officers a wide berth as they walked toward him. The landscapers put down their tools and sat down while the police searched the exterior.

What the hell? The police came prepared. This had to be more than a tip. Red thought of the conversation with Ross and whipped out his cell. Smoke answered on the first ring.

"The police are at the Big Lakes site with K-9 dogs. Claimed they got a tip somebody sold drugs from here. I'll be walking through with them in a minute; I got a crew of ten. Get up here."

"On our way," Smoke said and clicked off.

Pressure eased from Red's chest as the police officer walked over to him with the dog. He allowed the animal to smell him before they started walking inside.

"Excuse me," he said to the officer and waved at Ollie. "Have everyone take a seat on the ground. He turned to the police. "Can the dogs sniff my men first?"

The cop nodded.

"Have the men line up," Red told Ollie. The older man shuffled to the crew. Red heard the murmuring and

Erosa Knowles- Men of 3X CONStruction
Book 1

cursing. He hoped for their sakes they were clean, it'd cost them more than their jobs if they weren't.

"You don't think that's risky?"

Red glanced at the policeman standing beside him. "We do random screenings all the time. It's a condition of employment. At least they don't have to pee in a cup."

All of his men and the trucks were clean. The officer looked at him as his men went to sit near the trucks.

"Let's get started," Red said, breathing easier now that his men had passed.

Someone had called the owners. Mr. and Mrs. Frenche walked behind the police officers to ensure no damage to their property. More police cars pulled up. It was turning into a circus. The dogs had completed the tour inside and found nothing.

An officer from the security company they hired had shown up. The balding man breathed a sigh of relief. The landscapers and his crew sat idle while the police roamed the house and yard. Mrs. Frenche snapped at them to hurry up before the animals left an odor in her house and threatened to contact the Mayor if the animals so much as belched.

Red eyed her elderly husband. The poor man walked behind her silently as she berated everyone in sight, as if they worked for her. He and the police officer looked at each other and walked in the opposite direction.

The cool breeze soothed his frazzled nerves. Someone had sent the police out here for a reason. They hadn't found drugs. Not yet at least. But there had to be something.

Ross and Smoke pulled up as he reached the

courtyard. Red separated from the officer and walked toward them.

"What happened?" Ross asked, walking at a fast clip.

"The police said they had a tip about drugs and bought out the dogs. So far, they haven't found anything. You know how it is. Police and ex-cons, it's a powder keg."

Smoke whistled behind him. "There are at least ten police cars out here. What'd they expect, a poppy field?"

Red chuckled. "Must have. I have my older men keeping an eye on everything. And just so you know, Andre hasn't shown up for work in three days."

Ross nodded and walked up to Mr. and Mrs. Frenche. He was their P.R. guy. Red didn't envy his job soothing ruffled feathers, especially on the old bird. He breathed a sigh of relief.

"You okay?" Smoke asked as he cupped his hand around a cigarette and lit it.

"It's cool. I'm not good with dealing with customers or the police like you or Ross. I'm glad you guys made it because I'm smelling some serious bullshit up in here. Too many cars, for a tip that hasn't panned out. Yet, they're still here."

Smoke nodded.

They watched the police widen their search beyond the property. "It seems as though they are looking for something in particular," Smoke murmured, eyes narrowed. "We didn't work on that lot, it's for sale."

Red nodded and watched the police walk around searching. One of them waved and called for the dogs.

"What the fuck?" Red murmured as he stretched to see what the officers found. Ross walked out of the house followed by the Frenches.

"What's going on?" he asked them.

"I don't know, they just yelled for the dogs a moment ago." Smoke stamped out his cigarette and nodded at the older couple in greeting.

Red muttered a curse as he noticed some of his crew crept closer to the police on the other lot. He glanced at Smoke and headed in that direction as well. No telling how loose lips would be if he or one of them didn't run roughshod.

Smoke caught up with him, leaving Ross with their clients. "This is getting damn annoying," Smoke grumbled. "We need to find out who's trying to destroy our company before they actually do."

Red nodded, his eyes narrowed to the mound of dirt the police officers surrounded. He stopped behind the officer he'd been walking with on the other lot. "What's going on?"

The officer glanced at him and then back at the mound. "The dogs found something."

Red scowled at the back of his head. "I know that. What did they find?"

This time the officer didn't bother to turn. He pointed. "That."

Red squinted as Smoke stooped down for a better look. A finger pointed to the sky. He did a double take. *A finger?* Somebody buried a body? Smoke stood and they stepped back from the line. Instinct warned him not to pull his men from the scene. There were at least twenty armed police officers and ten ex-cons. He knew who'd be the first suspects.

In silence, they walked back to Ross who stood talking to the Frenches. Ross stopped talking at their approach. His posture changed as he looked at their faces.

"Somebody buried a body over there. They are getting forensics and another team out here to work the scene." Smoke said, pivoting to watch the police put up tape and push everyone back.

Ross nodded and picked up the volley. "It goes without saying they'll need some information from us about everyone who worked out here. I'll contact Ms. Connie and tell her to have any information available. We want to cooperate fully with the pending investigation." Even though he looked at them, Red knew the drill was for the benefit of their clients.

Mr. Frenche slapped Ross on his shoulder. "I knew your company had nothing to do with this fiasco. It's not even on our lot." He waved in the direction of the empty lot next door. "Anyone could've come up that road and done some foolishness. As long as they don't drag us into anything, they can do as they please."

"You're right, Mr. Frenche. We paid a security company to watch your investment when we weren't onsite. I'll make sure and give the police that information as well. It's possible security may have seen something." Ross sent the man an old school grin. Mrs. Frenche beamed, but Red knew she wasn't as gullible as the old man was. She'd follow up for sure.

"Honey, let's leave," Mrs. Frenche said, pulling her

husband's arm. "The television station just pulled up and I'm not dressed."

"Television?" The old man looked around and then at the building behind them. "I wonder if they'll get a good view of those large windows. Cost a fortune you know." He nodded at Ross.

"He knows, honey, he put them in. Come on, let's go." The woman pulled him toward the Mercedes and sped away. The police stopped them at the road and made them turn around. Red faced, Mrs. Frenche marched through the front door and closed it behind her.

"They said we had to stay here until the investigators released us," Mr. French said unnecessarily.

Ross nodded and glanced at Red and Smoke. "Shouldn't be too much longer. The forensics van just drove up and they're working over there now." He waved in the direction of the crime scene.

"Yeah, I hope so. The older man glanced in the direction of the house and then at the other lot with television cameras. "I think I'll go join my wife. If anyone needs us, we'll be inside."

"Sure thing, Mr. Frenche. We'll tell them where to find you." Ross waved the man off. As soon as he was out of hearing distance, he pulled out his phone and punched in a number.

Red listened as Ross informed their attorney of the situation. As soon as the media found out about the company's owners and workers, it would become a media circus. He hoped the company could survive the backlash.

"He's on his way. We need to sit tight and cooperate. Oh, that reminds me." Ross punched more numbers. "Hi,

Ms. Connie, I need a favor. Don't pass this on to Cathy. I need you to handle it personally." He filled her in on what happened and his suspicions before walking toward the house.

Red and Smoke chuckled at the shriek Ms. Connie made. They stopped laughing as the police officer who had walked Red around earlier headed in their direction along with a long-limbed Latino beauty.

Red sensed Smoke's attention and glanced at his partner, surprised by the interest he saw there. Maybe they'd get a break after all.

"Good evening, I'm Detective Garcia and you're familiar with Officer Green." She waved at the officer who nodded.

"Which one of you men is called Red?" She asked.

He nodded. "I am."

She waved him over to the side. Smoke followed and met her stare. Unless they handcuffed him and placed him in a car, one of his partners would be with him at all times. That strategy they'd agreed on when they started the company.

"I need to ask you a few questions." She looked at Smoke.

"If you want to talk to me, one of my partners or our lawyer has to be with me." He shrugged. "It's up to you."

She nodded. "Do you know a Felicia Barney?"

He frowned. "Felicia Barney? Is that Felicia from the Subway?" He looked at the detective.

"I don't know, you tell me."

"The only Felicia I know is the one from the Subway

in town." His heart raced at the thought of the finger he saw buried being the sultry firebrand. She'd led him a merry chase but in the end called him up for some sexual fun. It hadn't lasted long; she had other fish in the fryer.

"When was the last time you saw her?" She scribbled on her notepad.

"Felicia? Damn, it's been a while." He scratched his head and looked up at the sky. "At least six weeks."

"You sure about that time frame?"

"Pretty much."

"How can you be sure?" She pressed.

"It was before a charity event back home. I left for the weekend. When I came back she'd moved on."

"You didn't see her again?"

"I saw her, she worked at Subway, but she wouldn't go out with me again."

"Did she tell you if she was involved with someone else?"

"I knew she was involved. I didn't know who. It took a while for her to go out with me and then she called and met me at a hotel." He sighed. "I don't know where she lived, if she was married, had kids. I only know she worked at the Subway and we kicked it twice."

"Kicked it?" she smirked.

"Sounds better than what I was thinking."

She nodded. "Make sure we have a number where we can contact you, Mr. O'Connor and you too, Mr.—"

"Smoke," he said, smiling. "Just Smoke."

She stared and nodded.

Ross walked up as they finished. "I'm Ross Stemple, a partner in the company as well." She shook his outstretched hand.

"Lt. Garcia." She nodded. "I just asked your partners to make sure we have a way of contacting them for questions later."

"No problem." He handed her a company card. "Call our office any time and ask for Ms. Connie. I've already spoken to her and directed her to give you any information you need."

She looked at the card a moment and then back at the three of them. She nodded. "I understand our dogs sniffed your men earlier."

"Yes, that's right," Red said.

"What about you, Ross and Smoke. Did they check you out?" She wrote notes on a pad as she asked the question.

"No, we got here after they were finished." Ross looked at the other lot. "What's happening over there?"

She pivoted, took a glance behind her as the shrouded body was pulled from the ground. "Murder and drugs, Mr. Stemple. Murder and drugs."

Chapter 18

The hollow sound of Ross's footsteps amplified the mish-mash chorus of anger and fear beating in his chest. Hands braced against the mudroom wall, he forced his breathing to slow down, his stomach to calm down and his face to cool down.

Cherise would notice any unusual cues, and he wasn't ready to share. His face felt tight and a quick glance at the hall mirror showed hair spikes all over his head. He headed for his office, placed the files on his desk, and closed his eyes.

All three of them, him, Red, and Smoke, walked a thin line. For years, many thought the ex-cons would fail and waited for the crash. Few believed they could change and work inside the law. To defeat this new threat, it would take careful planning, stealth and luck. His goal: to fix it without losing one of his boys. None of them would ever see the inside of prison again. But, if he didn't work fast, blood would definitely be on one of their hands.

"Daddy!"

Ross turned, took a step and caught Nora. He pulled her tight, placing kisses all over her face. "How's my princess today?"

She giggled. "I'm okay."

He inhaled her sweet scent, innocence wrapped in baby powder, and blew a raspberry on her cheek. "You have fun today?"

"Yes, Cherise washed my hair and fixed it like the magazine. See?" She pointed to her head and turned so he could see the braids.

With her secure in his arms, he followed the sounds and smell of lasagna to the kitchen. Cherise warned him of her lack of cooking skills and bought things that could be cooked in the oven or quick on the stove.

"Your hair looks pretty, smells good too. It seems like you guys had a busy day." He leaned down and kissed Cherise, lingering on her lips until Nora pulled his ear. He winked at Cherise, who returned his smile but stared a little longer than he wished.

"Daddy, I read a book on the computer today." Nora touched his face as she told him about her day. He marveled at the changes in her. She still had her moments when she shied away from him, but the activities Cherise worked with her on, helped more and more.

He looked at the woman who held his heart. She frowned at him.

A chill of apprehension slid down his spine. "What?" he mouthed as his daughter continued talking.

She shook her head and turned back to the stove.

He stopped. "What's wrong?"

"Nothing big. We'll talk later tonight." She nodded at Nora.

"All right." He cupped and squeezed her firm butt.

She swatted away his hand. His stomach clenched as a different fear rose. Cherise had taken on Nora, refusing to bring in a housekeeper or to put her back in school right away. She wanted his daughter to become acclimated to all the new changes in her life.

The investigation to find her mother's murderer had

hit a snag. The boyfriend had been in a fight at a club and had spent the rest of the time in urgent care. The police were looking for other suspects and had visited him earlier today with additional questions. He had no new information for them. He didn't know Pam or anything about her situation. The interview had taken so much time, he had to postpone a planning session with his partners and Rubie.

Ross shoved all the problems with the business to the back of his mind, and locked them down. Determination burned fierce to focus on his family tonight. He could lose everything and still be happy, as long as he had Cherise and Nora. They came first.

Later that night, Cherise sat on the loveseat in their bedroom lotioning her legs. Ross walked in after putting Nora to bed and settled his hands on her shoulders, squeezing, massaging her tense muscles. He poured some lotion in his hand and began smoothing it over her arms, back and then breasts. She leaned into him. Her towel fell away.

"Thanks, baby, for everything you're doing with Nora. I know it was tough at first." He leaned down and placed a kiss on the top of her head.

Cherise nodded. Her heart skipped as the scent of musk and vanilla swirled in her nostrils. His hands searched and eliminated every knot of tension until she was boneless. Two callused fingers grasped each nipple. Her breath caught as he rolled and pulled the tight peaks, sending tremors of need straight to her core.

"You make this a home," he breathed near her ear. "I'm so glad you're here with me and for me. Never doubt that, Cherise. Even if I forget to tell you every day, never forget how I feel."

She smiled. "What's going on, Ross?"

His leg stiffened against hers.

"What do you mean?" The deliberate calm in his manner, so different from his usual what-now tone, gave him away.

She licked his neck and pulled his face towards her. It took a moment for him to meet her stare. She waited.

He sighed. "We're having some problems at work, nothing we can't handle." He squeezed her shoulders. "It's all good, baby."

Now, there were a couple of ways she could handle this. He was tired and she might be able to nag it out of him. But, if they were going to be together, she needed him to want to include her in the important aspects of his life.

The other way to handle his shutting her out was to address it head on, in a calm, mature and rational manner.

Bingo.

"One of the ways you know it's safe to share your heart's secrets is after you've moved the woman you love into your home and your life. You should know she'd guard your darkest indiscretions with her life. Since she loves you, she'd prefer to share your burdens, rather than see you weighed down with them. That's how you know when it's the right time to share and stop holding the heaviness alone, the right time to open that closet full of skeletons." She brushed her fingertips across his chest, hoping he'd understand what she was saying.

Erosa Knowles- Men of 3X CONStruction
Book 1

He blinked. "You're right, I'm sorry."

"Forget that, I'm—what?"

He chuckled. "I said you're right, get your sexy butt over here and let's talk," he said patting the spot next to him.

She moved closer feeling the heat rise up her neck as he leered while she inched forward. Warmth enveloped her and licked her core. How could he get to her like this so fast? Her emotions were all over the place. Happy one minute, furious the next, deliriously hot and turned on after that. He placed a kiss on her pouting lips and squeezed her shoulder. The fool was grinning.

"Let's try this again. What's going on, Ross? And why are you smiling so big?"

"I love you and I'm just glad you want to be more involved, that's all." He patted her thigh, and snuggled her closer. "The police showed up at the job site in Big Lakes yesterday."

"What?" She tried to move but he held her in place.

"Yeah, it was touch and go for a minute." He filled her in, explaining company policy and procedure.

"Poor Red. The woman they discovered was someone he dated?"

"Yeah, although dating is a strong word for what happened between them. It pulled something out of him when he realized she was the one buried."

"What do you mean? He wasn't still seeing her, was he?"

"No, not at all. But it still hits you hard, just knowing the person is tough."

She nodded.

"Who do you think is behind all this? I mean, you've worked so hard to build a legitimate company, and for someone to try and pull it down is crazy." She paused. "I hope y'all don't do nothing crazy." She waited for his assurances.

"Ross, that was your cue to say, 'naw, baby we won't do nothing stupid.'"

He smiled and hugged her tight. "What's foolish or stupid, Cherise? Is it stupid for a man to defend his home, his family, his money? How does a man look his woman in the eye if he allows someone to steal from him and does nothing to stop it, especially when it threatens to take food from the mouth of his children? We have different definitions of stupid or foolish, so I can't say what you want." He kissed her lips and pulled her close.

His cell went off. "Yeah?" he barked into the receiver. "You're shitting me."

Cherise sat up, concerned by the gathering anger on his face. "Shit, stay with him until I get there." He hung up and threw his legs over the side of the bed. He turned and looked at her. Sorrow etched on his face. "That was Smoke. Red just quit and is packing to go back to Philly."

---The end for now---

Erosa Knowles- Men of 3X CONStruction
Book 1

Erosa Knowles has a love for the written word. Originally from Miami, Florida, Ms. Knowles now resides in North Carolina with her teenaged son. Two older children are married and live in North Carolina as well. An avid reader since college, Ms. Knowles is one of those people who keeps her books as old friends and has re-read all of them at least once. Many have been read more often.

Writing stories, creating worlds and characters fuels her imagination. It is both physically relaxing and mentally invigorating. Although life got in the way and she had to postpone her writing, it is the one career she always craved. As a writer, her days are just as full, except now she is doing what she loves; reading exciting stories from talented authors from various genres, and writing the stories that tickle her imagination.

Please visit her website: http://www.erosaknowles.net for other titles. Also check out the Men of 3X Construction website: www.menof3Xconstruction.com
All my books can be found on Amazon, Barnes & Nobles, All Romance, and SittingBullPublications.com

Other Books by **Erosa Knowles**:

Reclamation – Murder at the Beach
Reclamation – Lies in the Morgue
Reclamation – That's Not My)
Letting Go
Lyon on a Leash

Promises Kept
Loving a Bad Boy*
Secrets
Special Forces
Nikki's Challenge
The Ultimate Breed
Have I Told You Lately?*
Ready for Love*
Where There's Smoke*
Not This Time*
Run to You *
Double Trouble *
Lawked Flame
Jaleesa's Pleasure
Jones Girls – Sabrina
Jones Girls – Melissa
Jones Girls – Angela

denotes Men of 3X CONStruction series

Erosa Knowles- Men of 3X CONStruction
Book 1

The Following is an excerpt from Red's and Denise's story, **READY FOR LOVE.**

Red sat in the driveway of the two-story brick home contemplating his next move. His partners in Three X Construction, Ross and Smoke, refused to allow him to quit over what they termed bullshit. He'd finally hopped in his Hummer and drove around to clear his head. At least that's the shit he'd told his boys. The look on both their faces called him a liar. Hitting the steering wheel, he yelled out his frustration.

Why'd he always have to be the fuck-up?

All his brothers had strong careers working for themselves. As the youngest, he'd had less responsibility and stayed in the most trouble.

Smoke had called him out days before for straddling the fence in his non-relationship with his babies' mama and ex-girl, Denise. She'd been right. He needed to grow up. Ever since the fundraiser a few weeks ago, she'd been on his mind more than usual. That was hard to understand since she was buried so deep inside him, she was never far from his thoughts.

The red sparkly dress she'd worn that night had his balls tensing and his cock straight hard. He lost his mind for a second when he saw her looking up at that asshole. Smoke had tried to stop him, but he was on autopilot. Nobody touched his woman. Fuck that they'd had a disagreement. She was still his. It was all he could do to keep from throwing her over his shoulder and taking her to a dark corner. He'd make her remember why they'd been so good together.

When he heard her complaining to Ms. Connie, the construction company's office manager, and Cherise, something snapped. She'd broken up with him on a bullshit tip and wouldn't talk to him. Lord knows he'd tried.

That was probably why he sat, like a lump of coal, in her driveway at nine pm. He had a shitload of mess on his mind and didn't want to be alone. He'd bypassed his townhouse, as well as Smoke's offer to crash at his beachfront condo. Now, like a jackass, he sat on the outside wanting in.

Pathetic.

That's what this insatiable need to be around her was fast becoming. He inhaled and glanced at his watch for the tenth time in the past twenty minutes, hoping to clear his head in preparation for a titillating exchange with Denise. She wasn't easy, but matched him perfectly. You'd never know she was a preacher's kid the way her mouth went off. Thinking of her mouth, led to visions of her full lips, which made him hard. He swallowed, pushing away his desire and righting his pants.

Unlocking his door, he stepped out of his black Hummer and pocketed the keys as he moved slowly toward the door. A car sounded in the distance, the hum of a neighborhood settling for the night calmed his jangled nerves. The mat proclaimed 'welcome.' Somehow, he doubted it extended to him.

After ringing the doorbell, he stepped back so she could see him. He suspected she knew he'd been outside the moment he arrived. It probably tickled her that he took this long to knock on her door. Probably thought he'd been scared. He wasn't sure how far off she was on that. Not of her, but the whole situation with someone sabotaging the company, his role in it and since he was being honest, their relationship or lack thereof, worked his nerves.

His hands stroked the cotton lining in his pockets searching for additional warmth as he ducked his chin into the collar of his heavy Burma jacket against the night chill. Light footsteps neared the door. Without conscious thought, he rocked side-to-side, digging in his pockets further.

"Red?" a muffled voice asked surprised.

"Yeah." Who the hell else would be showing up this time of night, he wondered.

"What?" The chain he installed rattled as she disengaged it. "What are you doing here?" She finished unlocking the dead bolt and looked through the storm door at him in surprise.

I need you to hold me and tell me everything will be okay. "I need to talk to you," he said.

"You couldn't have called?" she snapped. One hand held her blue fleece robe in place as the other unlocked the last barrier between the cold and warmth. She swung open the door and stepped back.

"Yeah, I could've called, but I wanted to see you and the girls. I hoped to catch them before they went to bed." *Liar.*

He relocked the storm door and then the heavier door before glancing at her again. In truth, he needed a moment to pull it together. Seeing her dressed for bed fucked with him in ways he didn't want to explore. Well he did, but that would lead to blue balls.

At five feet six inches, compared to his six-foot three frame, she wasn't very tall, but she'd been blessed with beautiful clear mocha-colored skin, straight white teeth, a fantastic set of high sitting, perky breasts and a nice round ass. He'd been drooling over her body for the past eight years. Even after the girls were born, she'd snapped back into shape and still looked good.

Damn good.

Inwardly he groaned. Looked like he'd suffer with blue balls regardless.

She nodded and walked toward the family room. A quick glance showed she hadn't changed much in the living or dining room since the last time he'd been here. The large rose-colored sofa and love seat dominated the formal areas with beautiful abstract artwork she picked out right before the girls were born. The familiar large dining room table and heavy cream-colored chairs she'd just had to have were in their normal place. Nodding he glanced to the staircase and halls, appreciating it still felt like home.

Muted sounds of the television program she'd been watching drew his attention. Bringing back memories from an earlier time when they'd stay up late watching the comedy channel or some of the drama crime series. Seemed like years instead of ten months.

He smiled. They'd had some good times. Stubbornly, he refused to accept they were forever finished. She loved him once; he'd make her love him again. First, she'd have to talk to him. For some reason, she refused to discuss their relationship.

"Still watching those crime shows I see." He nodded at the television while taking off his coat and laying it on the chair. The fireplace blazed sending warmth in the barely lit room to his frozen digits. He sighed in appreciation.

"This isn't a crime show. It's about a medical examiner, a woman. I like the stuff she does, how she solves problems." She clicked a few buttons on the remote and turned to face him.

"Okay, what's up?"

After sitting, he'd laid his head back on the top of the sofa and sunk into the soft fabric. This had always been his favorite seat in the house. He opened one eye at her.

How to play this, he wondered. Straight shooting didn't necessarily work with women in general and this one in particular. He glanced at her heart-shaped face and slanted dark brown eyes trying to gauge her bullshit meter.

He gave up, too tired and mixed up inside to think up something new.

"I quit the business tonight."

www.ingramcontent.com/pod-product-compliance
Lightning Source LLC
Chambersburg PA
CBHW061203170626
46809CB00003B/1222